CCSU

ENGLISH

The Connecticut Literary Anthology 2021

Executive Editor: Jotham Burrello

Genre Editors: Christopher Morris, Makenzie Ozycz, Cecilia Gigliotti, Anna Christiano

Guest Editors: Colin Hosten, José B. González, Sonya Huber

Readers: Janay Wynter, Claire Hibbs-Cusson, Danny Contreras, Daria Washington, Marina Capezzone, Julia Wnuk

Production Coordinator: Kristiana Torres

The anthology was generously supported by an anonymous donor grant, which was administered by the Hartford Foundation for Public Giving.

www.ccsu.edu/english/whyenglish.html

ISBN: 9781732414167

Library of Congress Control Number: 2021946127

Printed in the United States of America

Book Design by Jillian Goeler, Jag Ink

Interior Design by bi'tık creative

First Edition
10 9 8 7 6 5 4 3 2 1

CCSU English Department
New Britain, Connecticut

For All Connecticut Readers and Writers

Contents

NONFICTION

POETRY

FICTION

INTRODUCTION

"Literature offers us feelings for which we do not have to pay. It allows us to love, condemn, condone, hope, dread, and hate without any of the risks those feelings ordinarily involve." So writes Janet Burroway in her classic textbook—and though we don't have to pay in lived experience, the best writing resonates, creating deep feelings and pathos we carry around behind our masks. Each piece in this second anthology can trigger a heady dust devil. The work presents an emotional buffet reflecting our turbulent world: cultural realignment, racial reckoning, climate disaster, and a military defeat wrapped in a global pandemic. One bitter sandwich. One mega stomachache. And yet, we carry on seeking peace, grace, and joy. We must never forget joy. The writers deliver on some of these themes, though, while they reveal the pain, many times their own, they deliver understanding, and sometimes, joy. It's crisp and poignant writing from the Nutmeg State that will be felt beyond our borders.

The last two years, while we hunkered down in CO-VID-19-imposed isolation, I've been fortunate to connect with Connecticut writers. Thank you to the 315 Connecticut writers who submitted over four hundred essays, stories, and poems for consideration for this year's anthology. Our crack team of readers, genre editors, and guest editors debated their way down to the forty-two pieces here. After selection, our genre editors worked closely with a number of writers, sharpening the work.

Even under the best circumstances, publishing is exacting work. But living through a worldwide pandemic has increased the physical and psychic distance between us as the events and institutions that support the literary arts have gone online or dark. Writers work in solitary alcoves but thrive within a supportive community. I challenge all Connecticut readers and writers to support the literary arts' return. As live, in-person events and workshops return to libraries, colleges, and bookstores, reserve your seat. Mask up and plan to attend one literary event each month. Post your reflections on the festival Facebook page. We promote statewide events each week. Dust off your literary citizenship card as we emerge from the pandemic darkness into the new-normal bright light.

I'm indebted to the visionary educators who encouraged and supported our team during the production of the anthology: Melissa Mentzer, Aimee Pozorski, and the entire English faculty at Central Connecticut State University. Tip of the hat to Robert Wolff, dean of the college of Liberal Arts and Social Sciences, and all senior CCSU administrators, particularly those involved in the CCSU Foundation. Bravo to the team at the Connecticut Literary Festival and our designer, Jillian Goeler. And to our anonymous donor, whoever they be, celebrate your wise investment in Connecticut writers. On behalf of all readers, we thank you.

The writers in the second anthology hail from Woodstock to Ridgefield, from Windsor Locks to New Haven. It's a diverse ensemble. Thank you to the all the writers who trusted us with their work, and a hearty congratulations to the writers whose work you hold in your hands.

Jotham Burrello
September 2021
New Britain, CT

NONFICTION

Raggies: A Natural History

by Kathryn Fitzpatrick

"Mount Raggie is somewheres over beyond Salisbury. I met an old farmer up there...I was walkin' along the road and I see this lad lookin' at this pile of bones over in his pasture. 'that there used to be a cow, mister, he says. 'that's all they left me."

—Ed Robertson, Thomaston, Connecticut, 1939

Cindy Garry's been a teller at Torrington Savings Bank for fourteen years. She walks to work every day in slippers, carries her satin kitten heels and her Danielle Steel paperback and her cigarettes in a Stop & Shop bag she's been saving on account of the plastic bag outlaw in Connecticut. She lives with her son and his son on Center Street, in a two-bedroom apartment above Sawyer's Bar, which she's never been to cause the crowd is too trendy, and anyway, she goes to the packy twice a week after work for her fifth of Dubra, which Sawyer's doesn't keep on hand.

Sometimes Cindy yells at customers. When they enter the lobby shirtless or pull pints of Fireball out of their briefcases or ask too many dumb questions or loiter for too long or want their cash back in too many small bills. Most customers at Torrington Savings Bank want small bills. Cindy yells at most customers.

Before, Cindy was a server at the Bertucci's in Simsbury,

in a plaza with an AMC and a Banana Republic and a Kiehl's. She still pronounces bruschetta with the crunchy *c* because she thinks she's class, and she makes it every year at the office potluck for an excuse to pronounce it that way. But Cindy's been wearing the same kerchief-hemmed dresses since '93, so when she whispers *fuckin' raggies* after the lobby's cleared out, it feels more like an acknowledgement than a slur.

Raggies live in northwest Connecticut, in the armpit between upstate New York and Massachusetts. If you drive around Torrington, down past Coe Park and the Cumberland Farms that always gets robbed, near the Knights of Columbus building with the monument erected for all of the dead babies lost to abortions, you'll see them walking. They snap cans of dip and spit into Dunkin' cups, carry backpacks filled with liquor and one-dollar bills rolled up in a sock.

They smell like motor oil or fried onions, the way a body smells when left to ripen for too long.

Think of the Melon Heads of the Naugatuck River Valley, who, left to themselves, morphed into inbred cannibals and would gobble up anyone who went too deep into the woods. Think of the satanic village outside of Lake Quassapaug, the miniature houses formed with cement and pebbles, built by a man who heard voices then killed his wife. Think of the spaceship deep under the waters of Bantam Lake. Think Bigfoot, cloaked by the Berkshire Hills.

Raggies are legendary—but not the mythic stuff of legends. Like Halley's Comet or a solar eclipse, raggies are the real deal, only white trash. Find them in any Litchfield County town that upward mobility passed over: Winsted, Torrington, Thomaston. Here, people keep piles of tires on front lawns, drape Gadsden flags over their porches. They might work as nurses' assistants or auto mechanics or grocery cart boys, and spend their wages on Joel Osteen DVDs and end-of-days meal prep.

The word raggie comes from Salisbury, Connecticut. Situated in the uppermost corner of the state, nowadays it's filled with mansions and horse stables and helicopter pads, and the area around Mount Riga is the site of summer homes where New York hedge fund executives go to feel a connection with nature. The homes are angular and white because it takes a lot of money to make a home look barren and cold. But in the early 1800s, Mount Riga was an iron-forging mine, operated by immigrants from Latvia and Poland. They lived in log cabins built into the woods, played fiddles, and did all the woodsy, down-home things one might associate with people in deep Appalachia. This is the part of Connecticut the Appalachian Trail runs through; the people, forced out, are still poor.

"Raggie" is a bastardization of "Riga." As descendants moved south, the word changed with the people. Became loose, became harsh. It settled into places with mills and factories, with jobs for the unskilled or illiterate. When the factories went under, the people stayed, and raggie took on new meaning as a catch-all for the white working class. The ones that Connecticut, as it built up its shoreline and summer homes, left behind.

Patti's Place in Thomaston is the place we work in high school. It's a window-front diner where they pay kids fifty bucks a week to peel and dice potatoes, wash dishes, and mix a broken hollandaise. Each windowsill is cluttered by the shit customers bring in: toy soldiers, framed pictures of somebody else's grandchildren, broken turntables and plastic hamburgers and vintage McDonald's Happy Meal toys. The regulars have been going there since it opened in the late '80s: Double Jerry, drinking his black coffee and shouting numbers into his newspaper; George Seabourne and Mike Burr, the Thomaston elite who can afford to eat all their meals outside the home because they no longer have wives to cook for them. There's a man who comes in every day for a birch beer and nothing else. He's been doing that for twenty years. Nobody minds.

We go to Patti's for the gossip, for the home fries griddled on a dirty flattop. We go there to figure out who's moving into that empty storefront, the one that used to be Vi-Arms Restaurant, and then a tobacco shop. Patti knows.

There's this running joke that Patti is the mayor of Thomaston because she knows who's having an affair or who had kids out of wedlock, who just lost their job, whose son got busted most recently for narcotics possession. Once, she played the Mayor of Munchkinland in a community production of the *Wizard of Oz*, but that was years ago now, and anyway, the cardboard sets were a lot nicer than downtown Thomaston. Someone's always drawing chalk penises on the sidewalk. Someone's always leaving stolen shopping carts in the neighbor's backyard. Everything here's closed. We go out of town for groceries, for clothing, for Valentine's bouquets, tampons and Benadryl and cans of cat food and printer ink.

To fill in the empty storefronts, the town put cardboard cutouts of Donald Trump and "Jesus Heals" signs in all the windows. It's like a movie where some natural disaster is coming, fast, *fast*, and everyone's trying to repent before the great flood.

The guys at Patti's always talk about raggies.

"They gotta be Polish," they say. "They're only Polish."

"What about the Leather Man?"

"Different *entirely.*"

Some people think the Leather Man was the original raggie, some prophet sent to warn us of the slow end of days. He lived in the state park on the far edge of town, in Leather Man's Cave, named on account of his living there.

Here's how the legend goes: The Leather Man walked across Connecticut eleven times a year, carried a walking stick and a suitcase and an axe. Shop owners left scraps of fabric outside at night, food and water and blankets. He made his own clothes. From the soft squeak of the leather, the shopkeepers could hear him and they'd make signs to hang in their windows that read, "The Leather Man Stopped Here."

Some versions say he was a French shoemaker who followed his wife to New England only to find her dead upon his arrival. Some say he was the son of a leather merchant who squandered his money in pursuit of a woman.

We tell romantic stories. We pretend life is charming and bittersweet.

I grew up with the word raggie bouncing off high school hallways. It was an everyday word, a recognition of mutual poverty, a sharp jab at circumstances that stuck us all here like gum to a desk. There were sixty of us in the graduating class, just over three hundred in the school, and we all had plans to make it big, or at least move clear across the state, to a town with a McDonald's or a strip mall.

There was this running joke among some of us, something like, "You know your life's not that bad if you're not walking across the bridge on Route 6." That was the worst thing—to be a downtown walker marching up the highway toward the next town. Maybe we knew we'd all grow old here, and car ownership was the consolation prize that kept us hopeful.

During Spirit Week, we had "Raggie Day." We borrowed our fathers' work clothes— overalls and plaid flannels—fashioned togas from leather scraps and potato sacks. Some of us wore house dresses and gray wigs. We blacked out our teeth, wrapped water bottles in paper bags. We were garbage men and farmhands and out-of-work laborers and pregnant housewives. Churchgoers, waiting for tithe to pay off.

I went as my mother, a waitress. A third-generation resident of town who dropped out of college cause the money was good at the restaurant. She was a fine arts student, who, for years, told stories of her degree, how much she learned about shading and watercolor technique. She listened to Talking Heads to seem cultured, wore dangling earrings and patterned sweaters to seem artsy. It was only years after I graduated high school, and later, dropped out of college myself, that I learned she had never finished. The restaurant she worked at closed. She moved home. She married a mailman who played in the local men's basketball league and started a family and found a new waitressing gig.

She's worked at many restaurants. Each a fine dining place with a wine list and a small fork for salad. Each far away, like she doesn't want people to know what she's doing. The last one she quit 'cause she was the oldest staff member.

"I don't want people thinking I'm not going anywhere in life," she says. "No one wants to be oldest."

She's always pissed when I describe us as raggies, always brings up the fact that I never had to take the bus to school.

She says, "I was a good mother."

She says, "I did the best I could."

There are raggies and there are raggies; those who've settled comfortably into the lifestyle like a body in bed, and those who fight it, who deny it, who spend their life savings on nice cars and oriental rugs and beautiful, landscaped front lawns.

This is the truth: Litchfield County is dying. It loses people every year, to lung cancer and motorcycle accidents, to job opportunities in other states. It is hemorrhaging people like blood. There is nearly nothing left worth staying for.

Cindy Garry makes $14.75 an hour. She is sixty-seven. She will work till she dies. My mother divorced my father years ago now because he couldn't give her the life she anticipated. She used her divorce settlement to buy another house in Thomaston; we've lived here forever. It is the fifth house she's purchased in town, each slightly smaller than its predecessor.

Once at a bus stop, I spoke with a woman from Hartford. I said I was from Thomaston, near Torrington, and she told me I lived on the edge of civilization.

Once, I asked my mother about Thomaston.

I said, "Why stay?"

She said, "Where else do you expect me to go?" 🛡

The Place I Always Dream About

by Amanda Parrish Morgan

"Here," Thea said, stopping in front of a house on the corner two blocks down. "This is the place I always dream about. I can see it from my window when I'm sleeping."

She was zipping down our street on her scooter. I was pushing Simon in the stroller, trying to let her have enough freedom to zip, but not so much freedom that she might get hurt.

She pointed to a wooden arbor, white roses climbing up its sides. It was the kind of place *I* dreamed about, not literally, but I think in the same way she meant, when I was a little girl. I looked back toward our house, trying to figure out if there were any way she could see this far from her bedroom window. It seemed impossible. Still, I understood. She saw it when she was sleeping in the same way I saw honeysuckle and secret gardens and mazes made of topiaries from inside my own childhood bedroom.

A few weeks later, I was pushing Thea and Simon in the jogging stroller on a warm summer morning. We ran past her preschool teacher's house ("There's Ms. Dee's house!") and continued to a narrow paved path that runs between the town dump and the senior center. The path is bordered by chain-link fences on either side, dark, overgrown with garden-variety New England weeds, and only about a hundred meters long.

"This is a magic path!" Thea exclaimed. Which was exactly why I'd taken us down it.

One evening late that summer, we packed up for a family picnic at the beach. As we walked up the wooden boardwalk from the parking lot to the sand, she warned my husband Nick: "Be careful. Fairies live here."

"Where?" he asked.

"Underneath this bridge. They only live in places where it's dark."

"How many fairies live here?" This would not have been my follow-up question.

"So many. Thousands."

In "Childhood's False Eden," poet Louise Bogan quotes Katherine Mansfield's translator: "She had the privilege . . . of living in a fairyland, in the midst of a strange little phantasmagoria of which she was at once the creator and the dupe." Later in the essay, Bogan, who had her own troubled childhood, reminds us that "childhood, prolonged, cannot remain a fairyland. It becomes a hell." Bogan was referring to the way in which Mansfield's life, though it may have been marked by a kind of artificially prolonged innocence that seemed like a fairyland, turned dark.

It's nothing new to point out that fairy tales are dark, and although we imagine they were written for children, they are often cruel, sexual, gruesome. After Thea was born, I thought seriously for the first time about why fairy tales are this way, interrogating my own impulse to shelter my new daughter from anything even suggestive of suffering. It was my mom who explained that these stories are meant to be instructive. A childhood without loss, of siblings or parents, is a historical and global exception.

It was easy for me to tell myself my daughter wasn't yet aware of darkness, and for this reason, that I should continue to shield her from fairy tales, to avoid detailed answers to her three-year-old questions about cemeteries. I admit I have done just that. I didn't let her watch movies or TV until she was four, and we had never read from my childhood collection of fairy tales whose illustrated damsels in pointy hats were icons of my early literary imagination. And yet, in something that seems part a product of cultural ether, part inherited memory, and part collective unconscious, magic, dreams, fairies, and their underlying darkness are already part of the way Thea's making sense of the real and imaginary worlds she inhabits.

One of my favorite games to play as a young girl was some version of orphanhood. I was lost in the woods and had to survive on berries. I was fleeing a wicked city and had to use the scraps of fabric in the basement to make new clothes. This kind of game was only possible because I lived in a comfortable house with my two loving, healthy parents, but I've thought more and more about the ways that even young children begin to understand that someday they'll need to navigate the world alone. When I was a little girl playing at scavenging in the woods and transforming the child's things I had access to into tools of survival, I was mesmerized by books like *The Secret Garden* and *Mandy*. In these books, girls lived wild and sad, but self-sufficient, in cottages and gardens, surrounded by beauty they'd nurtured. *Orphan* is a word we associate with children, but most of us—hopefully, even—will be someday. A thing we try not to dream about.

There's a certain kind of space that gives me a haunted, satisfied, slightly frightened feeling. Sometimes the feeling is so strong that it's all I can remember about a place: the corner of a canyon in Saint George, Utah; a dirt road I once ran down while working as a field organizer for the Kerry campaign in rural West Virginia; the basement of the house we rented when I was seven.

Sometimes, though, these places are so proximal to my everyday life that I can seek them out on a weekend's long run.

I can update the memory of a dark valley on the edge of my otherwise bright, clean, suburban town and investigate: Does it still feel haunted? (Yes.)

There's a small private road that cuts through the street behind my physical therapist's office. Sometimes the easiest way to fit everything into a day of writing and child-rearing is to combine the trip to physical therapy with a quick run before my appointment. On foggy, midwinter afternoons, I almost always find myself making a familiar right turn past the Private Road sign, realizing that without planning it, I've ended up running past the overgrown tennis court (now so overgrown it's hard to tell if it ever even was a tennis court, though I swear I remember from some other run, some other year, that the rectangle enclosed behind this high fence really was a tennis court).

It's not all atmospheric with these haunted places, though. Even in bright sunlight filtering dappled through spring trees, the overgrown easement that was surely once an old country road makes the hair on my arms stand straight up.

When I asked my mom if she'd ever walked down this road, she knew exactly where I meant. "Something happened there," she said. I nodded. "Maybe just unrealized dreams and sorrow. But it feels like something more."

One year the juniors in the AP English class I taught went in together on an end-of-year gift for me. They bought the oversize hardcover edition of Carl Jung's *Red Book* released in 2009. We'd talked about archetypal literary analysis when we read *The Scarlet Letter*, and, I guess even more than I'd realized, my fascination with and confusion by Jung had made an impression. This class was small and intimate, made up of kind, interesting students who went on to become artists, activists, writers, therapists, academics. We'd grappled with the anima and the shadow together, individuation and lucid dreams, we'd used Jung's definition of dreams as myths on a personal scale as a way to crack open the novels we read. On the day they gave me the book, we pored over it together.

According to Jung, whose dreams, like mine and Thea's, were populated by gardens and orphans (but also snakes and demons and poison and water and gods and Christ), certain recognizable settings and characters and plots are so universal as to exist on a primitive, subconscious level. Jung believed all humans shared some, or all, of this primal understanding of symbols and that our visceral response to these archetypes is part of what connects us deeply to one another. Gardens, orphans, snakes, are the places all of us have always dreamed about. Which is why they are the staples of fairy tales and myths.

I'd heard that reading *The Red Book* would be disturbing, and it is. The book's chapters bear titles like "The Castle in the Forest," "Death," "The Opening of the Egg," and "The Gift of Magic." Jung felt he couldn't interrogate his own subconscious without the visuals that accompany the text, and writing about the book feels impossible without including the accompanying images. Jung was trained as an artist and the reproductions of his drawings are beautiful and frightening. These images were carefully scanned from Jung's original "red book" in a secret archive in Switzerland. His beautiful calligraphic German writing is reproduced next to his drawings. These drawings are of mandalas, trees, lakes, and monsters, and though they are images Jung recalled from his dreams, they are places and things I too have dreamed about.

Jung believed the personal version of a myth is a dream. Maybe this is why the place Thea always dreamed about, although specific, was also immediately recognizable to me. Roses, like the ones Thea says she can see from her bedroom window, with their delicate beauty and their dangerous thorns, adorn fairy tales, fables, and myths across cultures and centuries. When Thea said she dreamed about them, she did not mean she saw them in her sleep, having glimpsed them out the window before I tucked her in, but rather meant something broader, older, more universal.

In *The Red Book*, Jung recalls a dream in which he was playing with his children in a grandly decorated castle hall when a bird landed on the table, turned into an eight-year-old blond child, and said "Only in the first hour of the night can I become human, while the male dove is busy with the twelve dead." I wonder if being steeped in his own study of alchemy, symbols, and mythology so saturated Jung's life that his dreams *had* to reflect that worldview. And, as those who opposed publishing Jung's *Red Book* pointed out, there's something deeply invasive about making a man's private torments (Jung felt he was documenting his own psychological demise and hoped that in doing so, he might see a way to treat himself) public—it's voyeuristic at best, possibly even exploitative.

Whether Jung himself wanted the book published was the subject of controversy in his family and the psychotherapy community. It was certainly intended as a project to analyze his own torment, a dive into his own subconscious. After all the years he spent interrogating and often debasing his own intellect, character, and soul, in the book's epigraph, Jung explains: "the years . . . when I pursued the inner images, were the most important time of my life." He hoped that by writing through his own psychoanalytic struggles, in a sort of dialectic form that allowed him to be both patient and analyst, he might reveal (at least to himself, if not to the public) a greater truth than he'd previously been able to access.

Deep in the woods of northwest Connecticut, just off where the Appalachian Trail briefly cuts through the state, are the ruins of what was once called Dudleytown. The mythology of Dudleytown is outsize and hard to distinguish from the facts about a settlement that really did once exist on this rocky section of wooded land near Cornwall. Crops never grew, either because of the angle of the hills and subsequent limited hours of daylight, or because of nefarious forces. The land has been uninhabited since the early years of the twentieth century either because it is inhospitable or because it is haunted. Visitors are unwelcome, either because the ruins are on private land or because of secret occult rituals happening there. Blurring the lines between these two would-be distinct options are some strange facts. For example, the land *is* owned by a private organization, and that organization is called the Dark Entry Forest Association. The first time I tried to go to Dudleytown, my friend Stephanie's GPS malfunctioned and sent us driving in circles in the foothills of the Berkshires. The area is remote—certainly cell service must not be strong there.

In the weeks leading up to Halloween, No Trespassing signs line the roads in proximity to any trail visitors might use to hike, but the Spring day I visited Dudleytown was beautiful and sunny. We parked in the proper parking lot and did our trespassing only at the very end when we veered right just over a stream to walk about two hundred meters off trail. Sunlight filtered through new leaves and birds chirped (I'd read they wouldn't, that Dudleytown is eerily quiet in stark contrast with the lively woods that surround it). The foundations of homes, the town's church and school, old stone walls, are all still visible if you look carefully, but it's startling how quickly nature has reclaimed the area. A hundred years doesn't seem long enough to make a stone-built town nearly undetectable.

I'm sure Dudleytown, or any Connecticut trail, would feel different at four o'clock on a late-autumn afternoon, the sun red and dropping below the horizon already, but on this spring day it felt peaceful and interesting and storied, not haunted. I looked at the stone foundations and willed them into a place of archetypal loss and sorrow, but truthfully I brought that to the forest myself, and the darkness of Dudleytown's legend, the curious ghost hunters, teenagers, and believers in hauntedness it draws, are separate from whatever darkness may belong to the lives that unfolded on that land.

Last spring, I went to hear a local artist, MaryEllen Hendricks, talk about her Thin Places Project. She had asked friends and strangers to name a place where the distance between the spiritual and physical world feels thin and then photographed these places and printed them on silk. Before beginning a slide show of her photographs, she passed out little cards for us to record our own thin places. The first image she projected was taken in the same place I'd written on my own card.

I'd seen the orchard for the first time on a beautiful March day, tree frogs chirping, unseasonable spring like warmth in what was still New England winter. Although I visited the orchard with a friend, I'd felt profoundly lonely that day, that month, that year. Those moments, though, in the orchard, felt bright. And haunted. But a bright, open, sunny haunted.

I don't remember if my friend told me what he knew of the orchard's history or if I pieced it together later from online searches—just like the road with the abandoned tennis court, nothing dark or even remarkable, just an old orchard that was now part of a multi-town land preserve.

Hendricks never used the word *haunted*, and I know that in Celtic theology, thin places are locations of proximity to God—to *good*—which feels quite different from haunting. But the lines between my haunted valley roads, abandoned tennis courts, that frightening road in West Virginia, and thin places are blurry. Dudleytown did not feel thin, though maybe in some way its visitors, with their rituals and fear, might create a different sort of opening there. Maybe all haunted places are thin but not all thin places are haunted. There is darkness even in the divine, the spiritual, but not all spirituality is dark.

Summer turned to fall, and where we live in New England, the woods really do look enchanted for a few weeks every year. One late-October weekend, while Dark Entry Road must have been carefully patrolled, my kids and I were driving through a nor'easter on winding country highways to a farm where they'd be attending a birthday party. Just after Simon fell asleep in his car seat, Thea looked out from the back seat at houses built before the Revolutionary War, past roads with names like Gallows Hill and Musket Ridge. There were no other cars on the road when she asked, "Is this a secret place?" I think she meant a thin place. She was awed, not scared, and I knew she meant the road, narrow, winding, dark, lightly traveled, but I also felt something else in her question. Is there a secret in this darkness? I also heard, or imagined I did, the relief of seeing something familiar that until just that moment had been outside the grasp of memory.

Bogan's comment about Mansfield's prolonged fairyland made sense to me in one way before I had children—that being stuck in childhood after one had outgrown it was a sort of purgatory and a strange corruption of the order of things. After I had children though, I understood in a visceral way how tempting it is to inadvertently make that hell. Bogan isn't putting hell and fairylands in opposition, but instead making a more subtle point: that the darkness, what Jung came to identify as the "shadow," archetype, the awareness of loss has always already been a part of fantasy—even for children too young to articulate this darkness. And to deny children a way to explore that is wrong.

That fall, my dad and I took Thea to see a children's theater production of *Charlotte's Web*. My dad read me the book—many times—when I was little, and I'd watched the 1970s animated movie over and over again. We drove from Connecticut to Tribeca, Thea asking over and over again when we'd be in *New York City*. When the play started, I was alarmed to realize I'd forgotten something so essential to the plot: Charlotte dies at the end. Her egg sac and her writing for Wilbur are her life's work. In the dark theater, I turned to my dad, tears running from my eyes, and saw he was crying too. Thea shout-whispered, oblivious: "Where's Fern?"

Not long after we saw the play, I started reading the book to Thea, a chapter or two at a time. I was delighted by White's humor and vocabulary; the book felt like such a rare thing in children's literature: carefully constructed and smart but also innocent, sweet even, but not saccharine. Thea would ask all sorts of questions—why would Fern's brother be sent to bed without supper? What is *supper*?

The first time we read the book, I grew increasingly worried as we neared the end. I knew Thea hadn't understood what happened in the play but I thought that the intimacy of reading about Charlotte's death might make it unavoidable or even traumatic. Yet, after days of methodically reading a chapter or two a day, the book suddenly disappeared the day I'd thought we'd begin the final chapter. By the time it turned up, weeks later, we'd lost momentum and so started back at the beginning again. I read once that children often approach frightening topics like grief and loss by walking right up to what they can tolerate to understand and then backing away.

Thea is sensitive, especially about getting older. I know it sounds like I'm projecting, and because I myself have become so much more sentimental about aging since I had children, it's possible that some of the feelings I ascribe to her are either imagined or an unfair result of some subconscious anxiety I've passed along to her. But, since she was very young, I've noticed a deep-seated resistance to change that is more whimsical and nostalgic than stubborn. I bought her new socks—low-cut like the ones I wear with my running shoes but sparkly since she's four—and she refused to wear them. "They make me look like I'm in elementary school," she told me sadly.

After we almost finished reading *Charlotte's Web*, we watched the 1973 movie I remember from my own childhood. Thea started calling herself Fern and loved reenacting the scene where Fern sings to Wilbur. She asked me to do her hair like Fern's and for a dress as beautiful as the one Fern wears to the fair (as a little girl, I also loved that outfit, a pink dress whose sash matched Fern's hair bow). We've often walked to and from preschool with a stuffed pig in a doll stroller.

Like the book, the movie, particularly its soundtrack, has held up well, and like the book, the questions it has prompted have been mostly fun to answer. Why does the song at the beginning have parts of all the other songs in it? What does Wilbur mean when he says "we've got lots in common where it really counts"? Why do those men dance and sing with canes? She didn't ask any of the questions I'd been afraid she might: what exactly Charlotte was trying to save Wilbur from, where Charlotte goes after the fair, or even why Mr. Arable is carrying an ax at the beginning of the story. I wasn't even sure she knew what the word *killed* meant.

The other night I was cooking dinner and we were, as usual, listening to the soundtrack. Thea was calling herself Fern and Simon Avery when Charlotte's sad, wonderfully seventies ballad "Mother Earth and Father Time" came on. Thea said, "Mama, do you like this song?"

"I do. Do you?"

"I think it's sad." It is sad, which is why I like it. My favorite lines are "how very special are we / for just a moment to be / part of life's eternal rhyme." Of course.

"What do you think is sad about it?"

"The notes."

"But the words aren't sad," I lied, and immediately wished I'd thought of something truer to say by way of explanation.

The second time we started the novel, we read it all the way through. This time, Thea fixated on the scene where Fern's mother goes to visit the pediatrician, asking him if she should be concerned that Fern's spending all her time with animals she believes can talk. Dr. Dorian's response is full of admiring wonder. He says that it's not the writing in the web that's a miracle, but the web itself. And he suggests that it's likely the animals in the barn cellar really can talk, only adults are too self-absorbed to notice:

"I never heard one say anything," he replied. "But that proves nothing. It is quite possible that an animal has spoken civilly to me and that I didn't catch the remark because I wasn't paying attention. Children pay better attention than grownups. If Fern says that the animals in Zuckerman's barn talk, I'm quite ready to believe her."

White is gently (and like everything in the book, it really does feel gentle) mocking Mrs. Arable for her failure to understand the magical, full world Fern inhabits when she's on the farm, but he's also refuting her assumption that her adult perspective is the way that Fern ought to experience the world.

When we read that Fern began to visit the barn less frequently, Thea grew concerned. "Where's Fern?" she asked insistently in each scene where Wilbur appeared without her. "When is Fern coming back?" Although she's cast herself as Fern and sees the book as a story about Fern, here she saw herself as Wilbur, fearing that one day, I would not come back. Of course she's Fern to Wilbur, Wilbur only to Charlotte. My parents are Charlotte to me, an acknowledgment that the tearful eye contact I made with my dad had communicated. Thea didn't need to know the word *killed*—though I suspect she did know it somehow, even if I'd never taught it to her—to understand the inevitability of loss that saturates the book.

When "Mother Earth and Father Time" came on, Thea told me again that it was sad.

"It is," I agreed again.

"The notes are sad."

I didn't want to lie this time. I flipped back through rusty music lesson memory, trying to remember what it was about minor keys. Was the song even in a minor key? And what exactly was a key, anyway? Undeterred by my incomplete understanding, I offered: "I think that's because it's in a minor key."

This seemed to satisfy Thea, and then she asked, again, for confirmation: "But you like this song?"

"It is kind of sad. But sometimes sad things can be beautiful."

She seemed satisfied. I think she already understood what I did about the song, even if she couldn't or wouldn't fully articulate it. And, in that same way, she knows that fairies live in darkness and the path to the dump is magic and Gallows Hill Road is secret. The places we always dream about.

Intersection

by Victoria Buitron

I'm by the building that once housed a Lord & Taylor, which is now empty of the only moisturizer my skin tolerates and that prized cherry lipstick that leaves no stain. A store open for almost two hundred years. Now the edifice seems like an ode to a just-gone era of capitalism—time undoing an entity that existed when my great-grandparents lived but not one that would outlive me. All I can think about is the peculiarity of what used to stand—and what I would purchase—in the place I'm receiving the shot that will lead to eventual collective resurgence. An azure cashmere sweater worn twice that creatures destroyed. A black-on-black tuxedo jacket with a notch lapel and silver cuffs for our wedding night. Faux leather knee-high boots that strained my toes when I had no car, not realizing the pressure would squeeze my nails until blackened and loose. Then just skin, no sheet of keratin for months. This is what swirls in my head as I wait in the driver's seat, mask on, during an April that clings to rough winds reminiscent of January, an instant away from receiving the first Covid-19 vaccine. The only vaccine I've actually wanted to get since I was a teen heading to the Amazon. That one-time pinch was for yellow fever, since I would be exposing myself to thirsty mosquitoes. This time it's the first of two shots to halt a worldwide pandemic.

In the days leading up to Christmas 2020, just a few weeks before the building shuttered its doors, I entered the store to see if the discounts were worth it. No open fitting rooms, a mask mandate, and few heels left in my size six feet. Most of the gifts under the tree were bought during that outing: peel-off gooey facemasks, a teal cashmere sweater, Clinique goodies, light-pink ballerina flats, and a chestnut-colored choker. As I tried on a pair of heels in the store for the last time, I remembered my mother taking me there as a kid. I'd bring a toy and watch her as she ignored my heavy sighs. At least at the mall, Barbies in boxes entertained me while she shopped, or window-shopped, but at Lord & Taylor there was nothing.

This is how it was until I got older. Then I'd go alone after work, finally understanding why my mother ventured there, but I could only afford purchases during the Labor Day sale. Sometimes I would go just to pass the time, spritzing on some perfume that lacked a flowery scent. I'd linger to the men's cologne section to inhale the smell of wood, almost alcohol, or the musk of rain on sand. I didn't need to buy anything, I just needed to be there, and to not think of anything but what was in front of me. As a child this place inhabited nothing of interest to me, but as a young adult it was an escape. Then, in the midst of profound change and seclusion, it became a void. I pictured the inside only holding abundant grime, a mound of dust bunnies, or maybe abandoned mannequins.

In the parking lot, none of us leave our vehicles to head inside the building. No standing in line under bright lights, no last-minute trinkets to compel us into adding more bucks to our total price. The people making sure we get what we need are wearing military camouflage coats and pants, double masks, and some of them have beanies on to warm their ears. I take a photo of the building's exterior, the black font and semi-script logo still present, and wonder if getting a vaccine where a store once stood is really as much of a contradiction as it initially seems. It dawns on me that this nation has too often conflated essential services with entrepreneurship. A free vaccine is only temporary, enough to restart the economy and to bring us back to when people would comfortably cough into hands instead of elbows. We are all there not just to revive the monotony of our lives, but with the hope to soon fill up the spaces we've abandoned: malls, mom-and-pop shops, movie theaters, or fitting rooms. A Lord & Taylor that has felt the wrath of all the stages of the pandemic is the perfect place to get vaccinated, then, and I accept the experience can serve as an Urban Dictionary definition for 'Murica.

Dense clouds in the background don't hamper the sun, and a fire department van that seems more like a golf cart idles by to see if people suffer adverse reactions. The first member of the National Guard who asks my name and age plays Bad Bunny in the background. It's the reggaeton beat and Spanish lyrics that convince me this is where I was destined to get the shot. After my car weaves in and out of more lanes, another camouflage-clad worker asks about possible allergies. She then swabs some alcohol on my left arm and introduces the needle deep into muscle, and although it isn't possible, it goes in so far I'm curious whether she touches bone. Take care of yourself, she says. My voice cracks and wavers when I say thank you. The relief pervades my body, and she leaves as quickly as she pokes me, walking to the booth to get the paperwork for the next car. I pass two more lanes, and in the last one, a man places a red cone on top of my car with a scribbled 9:09 on it, indicating the precise time I approached him.

In the minutes of wait, nostalgia overcomes me. There are no cars in front of me to thwart my parking lot views, just to the side. The surrounding trees have scarce leaves and it's too frigid to put the window down. Workers drive around wiping cones, erasing previous times, communicating on walkie-talkies, and leading a car that mistakenly ends up in the post-vaccine area back to the initial waiting line. No more metal chairs by the entrance for annoyed spouses and bored children. No food trucks stationed with tender truffle fries. Just a few feet away, some years ago, I had a Bloody Mary while searching for a crop top, when the thought of a pandemic only occurred in novels and science fiction films. While reminiscing I put my vaccine card in a cyan wallet, then remember that this is where I bought it. The t in "Kate Spade" is lost, maybe hiding in the expanse of my car or as a speckle in my purse. This place will now elicit dichotomous memories. One of capitalistic pick-me-ups that accrued over the years of my life, and another that encompasses the surge of hope knowing an end to an era of death and affliction is near. A man asks me, muffled behind his mask, how I feel. Fine, I say. He points to the exit.

It's 9:29, and as my car speeds away, I question whether I'll ever be back to this location for something other than a vaccine. Years ago, while posing in dresses in the fitting rooms, I never imagined that here is where I'd come to receive a vaccine to stop a pandemic that would have, by its one-year anniversary, taken so much from me and everyone around me. But who knows? This spot, with its remnants of a once-sturdy enterprise and harbor of personal memories, may be a site that I'll visit again, and perhaps it'll come to accommodate a bizarre moment that now—in my inability to see the future—can only be considered unfathomable. 🐾

Birdland

by Regina S. Dyton

We laughed! We laughed like somebody with no home training, laughed through our oppression and everybody else's living in Birdland. We laughed racism right into our innards, sexism too. We laughed at people's disabilities, addictions, economic injustice, mental illness, mean-ness, traditions and religions, poverty—even death! We laughed up and down Trent and East Hanover Streets, and especially on our way to downtown Trenton. We laughed at the stores where poor people shopped. "Your momma shop at John's Bargain Store." We laughed at how people danced, talked, walked, and especially when they fell!

Mornings, from the very last seat on the school bus, we sniggled, sometimes mean, at Veronica Johnson's wig in seventh grade. Veronica was a thin caramel-colored thirteen-year-old girl with saucer eyes, a cute round African nose, and full lips that looked as if they were puckered. She wore a reddish-brown wig, Diana Ross style, that fell just below her ears. My best friend, Ella, would whisper "Wiglet wiggie" and sniggle her mean sniggle, "Hnn, Hnn, Hnn." I didn't want to sniggle at Veronica but I returned a lighter "Mnnn, Mnnn, Mnnn" while secretly wondering why a thirteen-year-old was wearing a wig.

Then there were those explosive laughs that you had to hold in till they busted out! Those got my little brother, Joe, and I sent from the dinner table back into the shed just off the kitchen. When our parents weren't looking Joe would mouth "Daddy got a football head." Then we would both blow up our cheeks with uncontrollable vindictive anger laughs. It felt so damned good!

"Just git from this table until you can come back and act civilized," my mother ordered. "You just act like something *wild*!" We didn't care. We were laughing at Daddy. It was the only time I wasn't scared of him. When we went to the shed, we laughed out loud. Joe was afraid of everything from Jack in the boxes to loud trucks but with me in the shed, he felt safe. The light reflected off his little round head of closely shaved hair. For some reason Daddy never got up to beat us and make us come back to the table—probably too greedy eating potato salad, pork chops, and corn.

Trent Street. What a lucky place to live! Our house was on the path that Aunt Rose, Tookie, Miss Lisa, Sheila, Henry, Pete, Chally Bowles, Mr. Jimmalee, Aunt Lou, and Mr. Decatur took to the Big E every day. The only ones who didn't take the path were Uncle Clarence and the Peters. Uncle Clarence hadn't walked in years due to a stroke. He sat on his bent aluminum and green plastic woven chair. His dingy-yellow leather-looking cast stank. He gnarled out words while he dug spastically into his dirty pocket. "Hey, gal . . . gggoooo, bbbring me aaa a half pint."

Without words, I was taught that it was only polite to laugh at ourselves. As the West African saying goes, "I am because we are." Helen, Cynthia and Tookie, Chally, Hezzie, Sheila, Pete, Henry, Aunt Rose, Aunt Lottie, Twig, the Gilmores straight out of the Georgia fields on that rickety truck, Debbie pee-the-bed and Hook, named for the shape of his head, Mr. and Mrs. Peters, nontalking Lamar and skinny Andre. We were a people, a village, a tribe.

Chally Bowles got drunk—*every day* and stumbled down the street. He was short with a mottled-brown complexion due to years of drinking. The whites of his eyes were brownish and yellow like his teeth. We waited in front of our houses when we saw him at the corner, and when he got near our houses we'd go on the porch and kind of hide as much as you can hide behind those woven, aluminum lawn chairs. Sometimes the hot chair would scald us like a hot comb that nicks your ear. Some days we'd get lucky and Chally Bowles would fall flat on our eight-by-five lawn and Ella, Joe, and me just rolled! Flies would buzz around his eyes and mouth and we would laugh so loud my mother would holler. "Come get in this house right now! That is *not* funny, it's very sad. Somebody need to pray for that man."

"Yes, Mommy." Getting caught meant we were inside for the rest of the day. It seemed worth it. We'd sneak to the window for another sniggle but he was usually gone. Looking back, I guess my mother called somebody to come get him. Chally Bowles wore his suffering like a new shirt.

Everybody helped take care of Cynthia and Helen but we still laughed at them. Helen had what they used to call mental retardation and so did her daughter Cynthia. They were both the color of honey. Their eyes were large, light brown and always seemed to be looking beyond everyone and into the clouds. They constantly had a hazy expression, as if they were wondering about something. While we laughed, we were dedicated to making sure nobody came to take Cynthia away. No social worker better dare come into Birdland. Though solidly in the city, there was a feed factory and railroad tracks at the bottom of the street and our four blocks had more pigeons than New York.

My friend Ronnie and I would see them walking like two penguins holding hands down Trent Street. Ronnie said, "Helen, take that coat off that girl, its summertime and hot as hell out here." Ronnie often acted as their volunteer caregiver and guardian, strictly stating what others whispered.

Helen stared at me. She took a long time to think about what she was going to say. Finally she said, "Okay, Ronnie. Cynthia, baby, let's take off our coats."

Ronnie said, "White people see you dressed like that, they gonna take Cynthia away and lock you up in the state hospital." Helen laughed in response with her slow, guttural, hee, hee, hee.

We laughed at everybody we were afraid of.

Aunt Rose marched down the street wearing a housedress in one of her spells. She always had her knife. She was short and round, about as wide as she was tall. She would stop about twice every block and throw the knife in the dirt next to one of the curbside trees before the city cut them all down. Catching the light, her spinning knife shone until it blurred like when you look right into the sun, and in a quick moment, it was in the ground. "Taught you to fuck with me, motherfucker," she cursed at no one. Aunt Rose was Ella's aunt but we all called her Aunt Rose. Ella was the most afraid of her. She'd whisper to me, tears in her eyes, "Come on, Aunt Rose is coming, Aunt Rose is coming, hurry, it's Aunt Rose!" I'd go over to Ella's porch and we'd hide behind the chairs. She'd squeeze till her nails dug into my palm and then I'd start to sniggle for her; she was crying. Pretty soon she'd start to laugh until we laughed together. But we whispered sniggles when we heard Aunt Rose approach the tree in front of her house. She stabbed the ground. Then she would retrieve her knife and continue her routine, around the corner to the Big E Liquor Store.

The Big E delivered liquor to Mrs. Peters and her son. Another store delivered their food. Everybody was scared of the Peters. Mrs. Peters was a tiny, bony, bent woman, so wrinkled and dry I thought a good breeze would blow the skin off her skeleton. They never went past their front porch except for the one time Mr. Peters came running to the sidewalk chasing a rat that escaped their house, like he was trying to bring it back. His hair and fingernails were long and yellow; he and his mother had both turned yellow. They were supposed to be white but they turned yellow. She always wore a long white dress and he always wore white hospital pajamas and they both had yellow stains on the front and in the butt. Boys would go look in their windows, knock on the door and run away, laughing. I laughed from my steps across the street.

All of the houses on my block of Trent Street were identically built. Two brick houses connected by a common wall, then a narrow driveway that two families shared, taking turns and moving cars to accommodate one another. The Peters' grass grew as long as nature allowed. Every once in a while some neighbor would get sick of it and sickle it down before being able to mow it. The long grass was often burnt and dry in the summer. Their porch was dusty and bare for lack of sweeping and lack of use. You could smell the baked dirt on the porch when you walked past their house, or maybe that smell came from inside. The blinds were always closed but you could see that they were dirty and no hint of light ever shone through their windows.

While my mother taught us plenty of good manners, I often heard her laughing at the same people with her friends, on the porch or on the phone. She never laughed mean though, kind of good humored. She would help anybody. She told us all kinds of funny stories about growing up in Kentucky, like how when somebody was real sick they would call Miss Nanny 'cause there was only one doctor in all of Hart County. When my great-grandfather was dying, Miss Nanny would come over every morning and feel his feet and tell my grandmother, "Lula, he's dyin'—feets cold, he's dying." Her final announcement was always, "Call the Hi-talian; he's dead." I still don't know that doctor's name, just that he was a "Hi-talian."

Nothing was sacred. No one was spared on Trent Street, including the neighborhood queers.

Miss Lisa took her place on Trent Street as the court jester, switching down the street, both hips and one arm quickly swinging. She opened and closed her mouth with each chew and smack of her bubble gum, rhythmically, in meter with her walk. She was the color of a penny and had the profile of the Indian head on the nickel. She straightened her hair like Helen, just over the top, nappy underneath, and never curled it. She wore heavy pancake makeup and often a scarf tied like a bandanna while just hanging around the neighborhood. Miss Lisa preferred wigs for going out to church and dates. Poor thing had a huge Adam's apple that she sometimes tried to hide with a chiffon scarf or a turtleneck. When she was very young, Sheila, her sex-worker sister, let her wear her outgrown clothes until Miss Lisa joined her in the workforce, working for her big brother, Henry, and could buy her own clothes.

One day she staggered down the street bent over and holding her stomach, complaining of menstrual cramps. That's how I learned about having a period before the sixth grade movie or my mother getting around to the subject. Miss Lisa staggered up Ella's porch steps. "What's wrong?" we asked. She stood straight up and looked down at us with the most serious expression. "Girls, this will happen to you! The blood will run all down your laaiiigs." She bent over again. "And ooowww, oooh, the pain." Few could easily understand what she was saying due to a severe speech impediment. We not only laughed at her speech impediment, we learned it. It became our secret language. (If Miss Lisa and Ella weren't dead, I'd be speaking Lisa-speak with them today. Every once and a while when I go home to Trenton, I see Ella's sister, Carol, and we go right into Lisa-speak.)

We laughed our way out of church. Miss Lisa loved the Lord and she loved church. She joined choir after choir until someone told that she was a man in a dress and they kicked her out. But the street took her in.

The summer I was fourteen we settled for a tent revival because Miss Lisa still wanted a church home. A church that would pack up and leave at the end of summer would have to do for a faggot and her two ghetto friends. The tent church was led by a white, beet-faced preacher, Reverend Hollbrook. He seemed to be at the start of a long moneymaking career of passing the plate to collect poor folk's money. His hair was black and parted on the side, like all of the white men on sitcoms in the fifties and sixties. He was comfortable leading a tent full of Black people and ordering around the ushers, who really seemed more like security guards.

His tent church was just down the block and across the street from the Big E Liquor Store. Miss Lisa wore her purple dress and her red Tina Turner wig. On the way to church we sang "High Heel Sneakers":

Put on your red dress, baby

Cuz we goin' out tonight

Put on your red dress, baby

Cuz we goin' out tonight

You better wear some boxing gloves

In case some fool might wanna fight!

Put on your high heel sneakers

Wear your wig hat on your head

Put on your high heel sneakers

Wear your wig hat on your head

I'm pretty sure now pretty baby

I'm pretty sure we gonna knock 'em dead!

Inside the tent church we were shape-shifted from R&B to gospel. Good thing we were good at shape-shifting because we had to shift our asses back onto the street when Reverend Hollbrook requested from the pulpit, "Will the man in the purple dress please leave my sanctuary?" Of course, Miss Lisa didn't move. Months before Stonewall, she was doing her own protest all up in Jesus, rhythmically fanning and shouting "Heti, heti,

heti law Jeza" (Help me, help me, help me Lord Jesus). Two male ushers swooped down on her like prom queens wrestling for a crown. We stomped and shouted our way to the sidewalk, where we all busted out laughing. We laughed all the way down the street and into the bar. It was a valuable lesson. The church would put you out but the bar had an open-door policy.

The church was the only institution that put people out in my community. It was not the heart of the Black community to me; the front porch and the steps were my foundation, the heartbeat of belonging.

By the time I was a teenager, I was tired of laughing at everything. Ella still expected me to and I often played along. Ella started to drink when she was twelve. I still loved her. I tried to keep her company but it wasn't in me. We explored our bodies as they changed, going to her room to admire our new and quickly growing breasts, pubic hair and new shapes. She always had more hair than me but always told me how pretty my leg hair was while she rubbed Avon cream on them. Somehow, for reasons I still don't get, I started to see her sadness and to feel my own. We laughed together but we cried alone. I heard her at night, and I'm sure she heard me through the screens and across the narrow alley that separated our bedrooms. The bricks made everything echo and we often whispered to each other long after we were supposed to be asleep. The Figueroa brothers, two caramel-colored Puerto Rican teenage boys from East Hanover Street, made their way into Birdland to court a couple of colored girls. They serenaded us from the alley, doing their best to sound like Smokey Robinson. "Oooh, la la la la. I did you wrong," until our fathers cursed them out and ran them ran off.

I moved away to college in Connecticut in 1973 and Ella moved deeper into addiction. My letters came back when she was using; she was never in one place. She was just getting settled and I finally got one letter from her and actually talked to her on the phone. We were just starting to be girlfriends again when my mother called to tell me that Ella had been murdered. She had been stabbed 131 times by a crack fiend in withdrawal who was mad because she didn't have any money or drugs. It seemed that after three years clean, she had gone back out, relapsed, nobody really knows. We all thought that once she left her abusive lover, Rosemary, she would get clean and be all right. Her killer turned himself into the police twelve hours later, saying that Ella's words haunted him. "Why are you doing this, you know I love you like a son."

I cried at her funeral. I knelt before her casket and wailed until my mother picked me up because I was scaring her. I still resent that. The rest of my Ella cry is still inside after all these years. Miss Lisa had died years before. A "date" murdered her and was caught throwing her body into the Hudson River, where so many of our transgender sisters took their last breaths.

After Ella's funeral, her sister Carol and I laughed. We still do. We laugh about the old days and Aunt Rose and Chally Bowles. We laugh about Ella and Miss Lisa and how we had a tribe of crazy folks. The white social workers were too afraid to come to Birdland! We laugh at how we did the best we could to take care of one another.

There's no more mean laughter in my life. I'm not so afraid anymore. But the old stories still well up the chuckles, especially "Daddy got a football head."

He never laughed at Miss Lisa. He said, "Goddamn queers; niggers ain't shit." He said that at least twenty times a day.

Several years ago, at Thanksgiving, my mother told me that my father loved men, Yep, Daddy was on the down-low, but my mother found his closet door wide open. She said they never talked about it but she always knew, and even had proof. My father died at sixty-one, a miserable, diabetic, double amputee, self-hating Black gay or bisexual alcoholic who would not even *try* to take care of himself.

I wish he could have laughed. I try to be out and proud, Black and loud in his memory. I try to heal my internalized oppression. Most of the people in this story are dead, most did not live to see forty. After sixty-seven years Black, I look back with gratitude that I can still laugh. ◈

How to Sell a Used Subaru

by Lary Bloom

Step One: You sign up in the fall of 1961 for a college course called Introduction to ROTC, because, though you have no urgent desire to shoot anyone, you are a child of World War II.

Step Two: Four semesters later, you face a decision. Recovered from your first clinical depression after spending too much time acting in plays and writing features for the campus daily while neglecting to go to classes, you are given a choice: enroll in the advanced curriculum of the art of war, or play military roulette. If you stick with it, you must report for active duty after graduation, something distasteful. If you don't, you'll probably be drafted, something distasteful. But you are far from alone in this conundrum. This is because this is the fate of most young men who in the Cold War era have the misfortune to experience excellent health. And, as the son of veteran who didn't rise above staff sergeant in the Pacific, you'd rather begin your own military stint as a commissioned officer. Besides, there seems to be no Hot War at the moment. So you opt to stay, in part because the Pentagon bribes you with payments of twenty-seven dollars per month, enough to cover your laundry bill and Sunday editions of the *New York Times*, which your international relations professor requires you to read, as he expects you to grasp why the world is a perpetual powder keg, and why politicians don't understand anything, although that doesn't stop them from expressing their ignorance and sending young people to their deaths before going off on their golf outings at the Congressional Country Club.

Step Three: You receive, along with your bachelors of science in journalism sheepskin, a commission in the United States Army in the Quartermaster Corps, which relieves you, as it is a "noncombat" branch. You drive your Dodge Dart, the one you bought new for $1,976 because it was heavily dented in a hailstorm, to the American South for training and your permanent duty station, which turns out to be permanent for six months. During that time, you serve as commissary store officer, explaining to customers why the price of a half a gallon of whole milk has jumped from thirty-one cents to thirty-three cents though you don't really have a clue. And you are also given the additional duty of assistant mortuary officer, which turns out to be something of an omen.

Step Four: Because you have no say in the matter, you embark on an all-expenses paid voyage to a gorgeous landscape of the southern part of Vietnam that, unfortunately, is home at the moment and for years afterward to vile circumstance. There, in a country fatally divided by politics, religion, colonialism, revenge, hard economic realities, and land mines, many of your fellow soldiers, fighting a war that will be torn asunder by historians, are sent home in body bags, and many others will face years or decades of mental consequence. Your "noncombat branch" is suddenly the target of ambushes. As the convoy commander, you barely escape one of them because the AK-47 round aimed at your brain rips instead through the jeep's canvas top. (Had the sniper's aim been slightly better, he would have obviously rendered you ineligible to write this account.) Yet, against expectations, you survive your own eleven-month, thirteen-day, six-hour, twenty-three-minute tour with no serious physical traumas.

Step Five: You return to civilian pursuits, a member of a disgraced society of veterans of the most controversial war since that calamity started at Fort Sumter, and follow your nose for news as a newspaper writer and Sunday magazine editor. The war is officially over, but unofficially it becomes the source of nightmares so prevalent that you can't ever leave it in the past. In these nighttime skirmishes, you are ordered to return to Vietnam to do it right this time. But your boots are missing. Your insignia, too. And your fatigue pants. You reply to the commanding officer, "I'd like to go back to war, but I have nothing to wear." In real life, from your editor's desk, you publish stories of the war that conflict with other stories of the same cataclysm, because no one, not even the sharpest writers and academics (most of whom escaped military service) understand what happened or why, or what the true legacy may be. One story is written by a veteran who ordered an artillery bombardment that, because of his own error in calculating the strike, went astray and killed his best friend. He writes that he sees that friend again every time he goes to sleep, and pleads for forgiveness. In your final decade in the magazine world, you drive a car from your upgraded fleet (a Saab or a top-of-the-line Honda) on the thirty-five-mile commute from your small Connecticut town to the city where you work. One day, your publisher calls and asks you to take on a high school student as an intern. You balk because all of your interns have been college students. But, as the publisher signs your paycheck, you take on the girl, only sixteen. She is a native of the country that hosted your war, and after it, her father was sent to a reeducation camp for many years. Against expectation, the young intern is an instant hit with staff, not only because she brings her mother's pork dumplings to the weekly staff meeting but because she's a human dynamo. She organizes a writers' conference and persuades the likes of Arthur Miller and William Styron to speak. She brims with ideas for profiles and investigations. You become interested in her college plans. She says she dreams of going to Harvard. You ask her what kind of high school grades she gets even though you already suspect they are spectacular, which they are. And how she did on the

SATs—a perfect score. You opine that with her academic record, and because she is a member of a segment of the population that such institutions seek to promote campus diversity with, she is a shoo-in. She looks at you as if you are the mayor of Pluto. If you knew, she says, how many Vietnamese students score perfectly on the SATs, you wouldn't say that. In fact, she doesn't get into Harvard, and goes to Brown instead, and studies art, her passion. And years later, goes to law school, and then takes a job in a prestigious firm.

Step Six: In 2010, you buy a used Subaru sedan that has only thirteen thousand miles on it and drive it for seven years. Because your commute is long and your house is isolated in the woods, you and your wife need two cars. She drives a Saab wagon.

Step Seven: Having finished your tour of corporate duty and been granted a buyout in a failing business, you go out on your own as a writer and editor, though a friend advises you not to if you want to be able to pay for car repairs, and, perhaps, groceries. During this time you write some books, and a play about the Vietnam War, though it is not about you but about a childhood friend, a navigator/bombardier on a fighter jet, whose body was not found for forty years. After the play is staged, friends who see it suggest going back to Vietnam, a step most veterans of the war have avoided.

Step Eight: Because Vietnam has never left you, you decide you will never leave it. And you and your wife, not the wife you were married to in your officer days, because she didn't survive to the end of the war, but your final wife, plan an independent adventure in the place you once feared going to, in order to make sense of things. You savor, in addition to the street food in Ho Chi Minh City, fish stew in Nha Trang, the local beer in Hue, watermelon in Dalat, and innovative cuisine in the magical village of Hoi An, that the people everywhere are glad to see you. Among your souvenirs: a T-shirt that says "Good Morning, Vietnam."

Step Nine: Because you live an urban life now (you have moved from the little town to a Connecticut city), you and your wife no longer need two cars. So you put the Subaru sedan up for sale, though you don't look forward to the process. Your former intern, the native of Vietnam, whom you've kept in touch with, sees your Facebook pitch and says her brother needs a car in Washington, DC, and that her mother wants to buy it for him. Her mother comes to your house a day later, bringing a box of not very Asian homemade doughnuts and a mechanic who is also a native of her home country. He checks the car and says it looks worth the asking price. You take the woman to the DMV and wait your six hours until you can transfer the title. The clerk at the window looks at the two of you and might think, well, there's a nice couple. She processes the papers, and all's well.

Step Ten: You sit at the desk in your home office and consider what you thought was once a fine moral to the story of the collective Vietnam experience: that as a country the United States finally would learn from its mistakes and understand the limits of its authority, power, and right to bombard to smithereens other countries so that they can be free. You ask yourself if you are the writer you think you are. Though you've published books before, you never took on in book form the best story of your life. You ask, What did that war do to your mind? But by now, of course, having put down these words, you are on your way to figuring it out. ◈

You've Come A Long Way, Baby

by Holly Carignan

You will grow a thick, lifelong bedrock of fear and humiliation, a hardened, crusted sedimentary record of your experiences. It starts when you are four, at the community pool, on the slide, and the neighbor, a grown man, stands at the bottom with his arms open wide to catch you. Your parents beckon you from the pool and tell you to never ever do that again. You don't understand but you feel a hot, hot shame on your sunburned face.

When you are in kindergarten, a policeman comes to your class and warns you about strangers. You and your classmates line up and, one by one, have your descriptions written down lest you do not heed the warnings. The nurse notes a raised, dark mole on your right shoulder. You didn't know it was there. You later look at it in the mirror and decide you hate it. When you are in the second grade, a child you don't know is abducted from a nearby neighborhood. Your mother discusses the matter with the other moms at the bus stop, and they all cluck, tsk, and sigh. You picture sinister, thieving men pushing their way up from hell and through manholes, aching, ravenous, ready to pluck children off the streets. You cease riding your bicycle for a week.

You develop before the other girls in your class. Keith and Danny needle you at every recess; request a showing of your tits. That summer, a pretty girl, one grade higher, gathers a group of girls at the community pool to torment you about the hair in your armpits. Your mother does not permit you to wear a bra or shave, says you are too young. You start wearing shirts two sizes too big over your bathing suit.

When you are twelve, you are riding your bicycle to the community pool and a car slows beside you. It's a dinged-up Volkswagen Rabbit, its driver shaggy and filthy, and you think again of those men coming out of manholes. You make the mistake of looking into his eyes, into the tar pool of his molten core. His tongue practically lolls out of his head as if he is a stinking, overheated jackal. He speeds away. You continue to the pool, your pedaling reaching a fevered momentum. You are hyper vigilant, scanning front, back, left, right. When you arrive, your mother is already there, relaxing on a lounger. You, sweaty but cold, gasping, stay by her side, and you will for the rest of the afternoon. At the end of the day, your mother is irritable as she tries to maneuver your bicycle into the trunk of her car. This time, you stay off your bicycle for the rest of the summer.

When you are thirteen, your parents corner you in your bedroom to tell you that you are getting fat. You do something about it. When your period stops, your parents reverse course and try to get you to gain weight. One day, in the middle of school, your mother picks you up and takes you to the gynecologist. It has never occurred to you that anyone, or anything, could possibly go between your legs and inside your body. The gynecologist is an old man with glasses, face wrinkled like a pale raisin, his breath stale. You see a foreign metal device on a tray next to the bed and the old man tells you to put your feet in the stirrups. You feel cold air on your naked bottom. The man inserts the device, and it feels like he is slowly opening an umbrella, all spokes and cold metal, in your body. It hurts. A lot. Your mother later drops you off at school and you sit in class, shaken and white. You turn and glance at the kid behind you but don't know why exactly. He asks what your problem is.

You shrug, turn back around. You decide to forget, to stuff the day's events into that crowded wasteland in your memory where such things belong. The mist of a depression starts to settle itself on your skin like a sticky insecticide.

In the tenth grade, you're riding your bicycle with your friend Stacy. You pass a car parked on the side of the road with a man working underneath it. The man is on his back, his face obscured by the floor of the car, his fly open and his penis hanging out like a dead, flaccid eel washed ashore. Down the road, at a stoplight, Stacy, her face ashen, asks if you saw what she saw. You sputter out a yes. This is the last time you and Stacy will talk about it, but you will always wonder if that man did it deliberately. You will never know. Sometimes a mystery must stay a mystery.

The summer before you graduate high school and leave home for the University of Florida, a story about a serial killer in that college town makes national headlines. That night, you are filled with dread while you lie awake in your dark bedroom. You sleep with the lights on that night. And the next. And the next. Until your father asks you not to. Months later, you see the *Silence of the Lambs* in the theater and your dread returns. This time, you go to bed with a book light on, but the battery conks out and leaves you alone in the dark. Before you move into the University of Florida dorms, you have that horrid mole removed by a dermatologist who later calls to tell you that it is not cancerous. For a fleeting moment, you wonder how they will identify your dead body now but remember with relief that there are always dental records. That fall, you ride your bicycle to class and pass a wall onto which the victims' names had been spray-painted. Every day that semester, as you glide by, you say those names aloud, into the wind, like an elegy.

Before you graduate, you attend a reading by a southern author who describes Florida as a "penis hanging off the belly of America," and this amuses you. Degree in hand, you pack your shit, drive north, and wave goodbye to America's penis. You find an apartment, a job, a cat you name Pumpkin. You love that cat with every atom, every proton, neutron, and electron of your being.

One day, two years later, you find a note written on a ragged scrap of paper and stuck under your car's windshield wipers. It says, in a shaky pen, "We are from different worlds but we are the same." You accuse a man who has been pursuing you for a date of leaving that note on your car. He denies it, and for reasons you don't understand, you believe him. You will never find out who left it there, but one day you will have your suspicions.

Not long after you find the note, you go hiking with some friends, and you all go off the main path. You find the horn of an old Victrola in the middle of the forest, just sitting there alone. The horn is strangely bright and brassy in that wet forest. You and your friends marvel at this random discovery and circle it like you are in an *X-Files* episode and have just discovered a flying saucer.

Your back is tight and throbbing after that hike, but you haul your garbage out to the dumpster anyway, out through your sliding door and into the cool, silent darkness. You will wonder days later whether you had locked that sliding door before you and Pumpkin settled into your cuddle and drifted off to sleep together.

You awaken to a stranger, a man, a man shrouded in the blue light of your clock radio. He yanks you up by your hair and tells you that if you scream, he will fucking kill you. You believe him. You know immediately what is about to happen. He gives you simple instructions: turn here, do this, touch that. You think of these directions as steps in a how-to manual: it is all mechanical and you will do what you must.

You remember that Victrola horn, its random appearance in your life. How, you wonder, did it wind up in the middle of the forest? You question whether it was an omen, a sign of events to come, but you can't come up with a logical connection between a rape and a Victrola. In your mind, you try to draw complicated diagrams of the connection, make what seem like brilliant mental leaps only to find yourself hopelessly confounded. The man starts a casual conversation with you, asks you your name, your cat's name, what kind of job you have. You lie. You sense a sad loneliness in this man, a pulsing desperation, and you almost feel sorry for him.

The man makes you get in the shower, tells you to count to one hundred. He calls out an apology, his voice trailing—you know he is leaving. You count, and you hate each number as it drops out of your mouth. You shut off the spigot, tiptoe wet, scared, and weary into your room. He is gone, your sliding door open—the one you may or may not have locked. Pumpkin is in a low, tight crouch behind the television. You call the police. And the Victrola? Sometimes a mystery must stay a mystery.

There are squad cars, a swarm of officers and two detectives. One detective looks like Morgan Freeman, and the other barks his impatience at you because you cannot tell him what surfaces, besides your body, the man may have touched. You request that this detective kindly please stop, just stop. Your sentence ends in a trailing, bloodless ellipsis. You are dying infinite deaths in front of these men, these strangers. Morgan Freeman tells him to cut the shit. They cover your walls, bathroom doorway, and sliding door with fingerprint powder, bag up your clothes, your bedding, tell you to go to the hospital to have evidence collected off your body. Your body is a crime scene. Pumpkin twines his way around Morgan Freeman's legs. He pats Pumpkin's head.

Over the weeks and months to follow, you meet with Morgan Freeman at the police station to go over your story again and again and again. After each session, Detective Freeman escorts you out the back door and stands on the balcony, his hands resting on the rail, his foot propped up on the bottom rung, watching you make your way down the stairs and across the lot to your car. You turn and wave before unlocking the door. You will always remember his kindness.

Several weeks after the assault, it comes to you in a synaptic jolt: you know exactly who left that note on your car. You call Detective Freeman, and he asks you if you still have it. You promise to look for it and tear through your apartment. It makes you crazy. When you give up, you tell Detective Freeman you can't find it, but you know exactly who left it. You are sure. We may never know, he tells you, a tinge of sorrow in his voice.

You max out two credit cards hiring people to move your belongings into a third-floor apartment with a buzzer. Over the next year, you read about three more rapes in your former apartment complex. The police set up a female decoy in the neighborhood and find a man following her with his zipper undone and his junk hanging out. Always with the goddamned open zippers, you think to yourself. You are unable to identify his picture, but the DNA speaks for itself.

You attend the man's arraignment. He comes out in shackles. You hear them rattling with his shuffling steps. He looks like he just woke up from a lifelong bender. He is unshaven, his hair long, dark, and bushy. He is entirely unfamiliar to you, which startles you. But now—you know his name. You see a middle-aged couple waving at this man and know, without needing to be told, that they are his parents. After he is arraigned, you go into the bathroom where you nearly collide with the man's mother, who is exiting, and you apologize. You drive home and think of all the inane apologies you have made in your life and realize that it is not you who must apologize. It occurs to you that even the rapist himself knew this. You, too, from then on out, will always know this.

The rapist cuts a deal with the prosecutor and is sentenced to twenty-four years in prison. You will live your life, with or without purpose. It is yours to choose. You go back to the forest to look for that Victrola but are unable to find it. You will never find that note. You have grown tired of mysteries. You send Morgan Freeman a thank-you card. Pumpkin remains your truest love.

For a while, like clockwork, on the anniversary of the rape, you dream about the rapist. In some of those dreams, you are expecting him, sitting up in your bed and waiting. Oddly, it is not a feeling of dread that you have in these dreams, but resigned expectation. He is a part of your bedrock, whether you like it or not. The dreams, though, they eventually stop. In the last dream, the rapist is unable to get through that sliding door. He pulls, tugs, yanks, pounds his fists on the glass, but he cannot get in. His hands bleed. He crumples into a heap. As dawn approaches, he vaporizes like a vampire in a shaft of light. The rape becomes like an ancient star whose ragged light has traveled through great distances of time and space to reach you so faded that you barely recognize it. You feel no fear now, and you find this odd.

Ten years after the rape, you jog past a motorcyclist waiting at a stoplight. He looks you square in the face and makes an obscene gesture with his tongue. You envision him skidding over an oil slick and laugh. You stop, lift your middle finger at this man, and then continue jogging into the deepening dusk. 🛡

Finding Dylan Thomas

by Thomas Cowen

And you, my father, there on the sad height,

Curse, bless, me now with your fierce tears, I pray.

Do not go gentle into that good night.

Rage, rage against the dying of the light.

—Dylan Thomas, "Do Not Go Gentle Into That Good Night," stanza 6

If you're assuming this story is about a poem and a poet, you are correct. About fathers and sons, exactly. Living and dying, bingo. Still, you might be missing something. I was too. Like many stories, it begins as a couple holds hands on a sunny spring day.

It was the first real spring day of 2014, seventy delightful degrees as my wife, Ronee, and I strolled around my old stomping grounds at New York University (NYU). Tree buds unfurled before my eyes, and two birds seemed to follow as we veered west. We wandered past the Stonewall Inn and the improbable corner where West 4th meets West 10th before arriving at the White Horse Tavern. Inside it was dark with black tin ceilings reflecting off the mirrored bar. Dust specks floated through the air as they might have the final night Dylan Thomas drank here. A night when rows of whiskey bottles waited their turn below a "Cash Only" sign.

As I savored my Guinness, I told Ronee that my parents named me after Welsh poet Dylan Thomas. We'd been married 26 years and had two sons. She knew my every thought, everything about me, except the origin of my name.

"Thomas drank eighteen shots of whiskey before he collapsed right here on this street."

"Your father named you after someone who drank themselves to death?" Her voice peaked; eyes squinted as she asked.

"I'm pretty sure it was due to his poetry, but I guess Dylan Thomas wasn't the best role model." I tried to soften the blow, "it was probably no more than nine shots, and some say he died of pneumonia." Thomas's legendary night intrigued me the way horrific crashes do. *Was it eighteen or only nine? What does a human being look like after eighteen shots?* But that's where interest in my namesake stopped.

From our sidewalk table, we marveled at New York City on display: bikers peeling north on Hudson, and two cabbies screaming at each other in languages that lacked vowels. A couple walked by with matching poodles, the man wearing a Yankees hat, the woman, Mets. Those were the usual allegiances with interteam couples.

"They must have an interesting sex life," I commented.

"Hon, stop, get your mind out of the gutter."

"No, really, Mets, Yankees, they must fight all the time."

"We were all Mets fans growing up. Who did your father root for?"

"I don't even know. He never wore a baseball hat, at least not with a team on it."

"That's odd, in New York City all the dads rooted for someone. Mets, Yankees, even the old Brooklyn Dodgers."

She was right. We grew up in Queens, only a mile apart. We discussed my mother and father's deaths, both within the past fifteen months. I didn't know what killed my father, a Christian Scientist, he had never gone to the doctor. He, too, didn't know why his hip crumbled more every time I saw him, why he became paler and thinner by the visit. Whatever it was, I suspected the liquor hadn't helped. I knew it fueled his creative juices to forget his day job so he could write or work on intricate pencil art late into the night. Knew it ravaged his body and personality for decades.

I told Ronee about the time he stormed into my room after a night at La Stella on Queens Boulevard. It was a restaurant that time forgot: red velvet curtains, buttons bursting on the maître d's tux, and a corner bar for five. It was my father's weeknight spot, communing with people who didn't have children and a spouse at home. People not like him and yet so much like him, mourning lost dreams, seeking something else. He must have had a couple extra that night as I heard our steel apartment door slam shut, pots clank on the stove, and his throat clear as he walked towards my room. I took a deep breath as he opened the door.

"Turn that off."

"But dad, it's the ninth inning, two men—"

"I said, turn it off, you should read a book or study acting."

"Dad, I'll have my MBA in three weeks, and I'm only 22."

"Everything can't be business and sports. You need to be more well-rounded, or else nobody is going to care." I inhaled the sharp layers of rum as he stuck his face in mine.

"Get the hell out of my room," I barked as I leaned my forearm across his chest.

He backed off.

I was in the NYU cafeteria when I called home the next afternoon. My dad told me he had just returned from his first AA meeting. I moved out a month later. He never drank again.

I first met Ronee later that month at Spanky's, an Upper East Side bar. Over the next two decades, we built a life together with a condo, then a home, a first son Brandon, followed by Justin, five years later.

I took Justin to his first Yankees game on his second birthday. I paid $10 for the scoreboard to display, "Happy Birthday, Justin," in the middle of the fifth inning and "Yankees welcome, Justin, 1st Yankee Game" in the middle of the seventh. He wore a Yankees hat that day and I hoped he would become a Yankee fan like his older brother. My dreams were simple back then.

Justin was five when he asked if I also liked the Mets. Since I grew up in Queens, I told him I rooted for the Mets when they weren't playing the Yankees. He responded that he was going to be a Mets fan. It hurt worse than getting cut from the junior high basketball team, but I told him it was fine anyway.

Nine months after our spring afternoon at The White Horse, we were watching the Super Bowl at home. Our family had just moved to a new town. Brandon and Justin sat on the couch as a platter of wings grew a shiny glaze on the table. I had just pulled a bubbling pizza from the oven when Justin, then eleven, let out a blood-curdling scream and grabbed his neck. The pain must have shot up his hands, then arms and shoulders as it looked for a place to go. Ten seconds later, it was over.

"Are you OK, honey?" Ronee asked.

"Yessss," Justin responded, driving his head down as he answered. I didn't know if it was the pain or the fact the Super Bowl had been interrupted.

I looked at my wife and mouthed, "What was that?"

"I don't know," she whispered back and squeezed my hand, "let's keep an eye on it." I sensed concern in her voice, but minutes later, I returned to the couch and the last drive of the game. I put my arm around his shoulder, felt him pull away, and in that moment I understood his pain. "Dad," he said annoyed.

I remember it now, as I did the instant I saw the second plane crash into the South Tower from eight blocks away. Moments when life changed for reasons I couldn't yet comprehend.

Justin's pain went away and then returned with a vengeance. Six months and many tests later, we told our son he had Osteosarcoma in his cervical spine. His build was slight, and voice just above a whisper. Three months after his diagnosis, a technician rolled him into the largest operating room at Massachusetts General Hospital. It reminded me of a Vanderbilt mansion kitchen; shelves climbing to the ceiling, filled with supplies, and a flurry of activity around the center island. I held his hand as three nurses talked to him under the stadium-strength lights. He responded softly, thanked each of them, and asked if his stuffed Minion, Bob, could stay for the surgery.

We returned to his room, where wires and tubes hung, searching for a body. The dirt outline from where the bed had been was like tape at a murder scene, all were reminders that Justin might not return. We went to the cafeteria, ate breakfast, lunch, dinner, and rushed to the room right after each, jerking to attention every time a nurse opened the door, hoping for news that wasn't yet there. They returned Justin to us after dark that night. Doctors removed his right vertebral artery, half of his tumor, and erected a titanium train track in his neck that day. Five days later, a second surgery, his raspy voice just above a whisper, he thanked the nurses and asked for his Minion to be there with him.

Three weeks later, I sat in his hospital bed and watched the Mets in World Series Game 1. We wore brand new Mets hats with a World Series patch. We didn't talk much, just watched, smiled at each other before he fell asleep in the sixth inning. Tears filled my eyes as I watched the rest of the game.

Weeks later, he was back on chemotherapy, throwing it up, then clenching his teeth ready for more. Screams in the night, two, three o'clock in the morning as the pain poked its way through the morphine, like a pitchfork. Then it was on to radiation, and I watched as his head was placed in a mask and screwed to a gurney like Hannibal Lecter. For six straight weeks, I sat in the next room and prayed the radiation wouldn't miss. It was all I could do. Still, he sucked it up like the batter trotting to first base after a ninety-five mile an hour fastball in the ribs. His was a quiet rage, but he raged against it all.

On a Wednesday evening, four months later, I glanced back and forth at a monitor as Justin's heart rate surged, then plummeted. I held his hand and watched his chest rise and fall. I motioned, raising my eyebrows, for Brandon to come to the bed. Ronee sat on the couch, looked up at her husband and two sons.

"I'll call for the doctor," I told her.

The nurse came first, then the doctor, moments later. The doctor was a resident, young, looked like someone you might sit next to at a Buffalo Wild Wings watching college football. He checked Justin's pulse, his wrist, his neck, then his wrist again. The resident tipped his head towards the nurse, and she turned the vitals screen towards the wall.

As if in meditation, I followed his labored breath. The same breath that had once given him the wind to run effortless 5k's and yell for a Mets home run, now slowed to a handful a minute. Slow, I watched, wondering if each exhale would be followed by an inhale. I kissed Justin's forehead, not wanting my lips to release. "I will love you always and forever. Always and forever." And then he was gone.

It was 10:30 PM. He battled for fifteen months, but he went gently with no last gasps or cries in the end. There was no suffering in my son's final moments. He had suffered so much already. We sat with Justin for the next several hours, comforting one another the best we could. The nurse said we could stay the night, but we decided to drive home at two in the morning. I wasn't sure if once I got home if I could ever leave the house again.

Over the next year, family and friends shed like trees preparing for winter. Several weeks after the first anniversary of Justin's death, Brandon went off for his freshman year of college. We became premature empty nesters with three vacant bedrooms and two acres with no one to play on them. During those nights, in the white house with the peeling paint, Ronee and I ate what we could and watched as a jar filled with corks, reminders of the night before, what was and what should have been. "Valium is like having wine," my doctor said. So, I opted for a glass, which became two some nights, then three. At night, I'd wake with my head throbbing, my mouth dried like sand, choking for a sip of water. When I couldn't go back to sleep, I would pull up the shades and read in the moonlight. Thirty minutes on the Pacific Crest Trail with Cheryl Strayed or fly fishing in Montana with Norman Maclean. My mind was looking to go anywhere, but a hospital with machines lighting up like it was the Fourth of July.

Then one morning, I wrote my first sentences. Wine pounding my head, pain in my heart pushed onto the page. The words hard, clinical as they relived the surgeries, screams, and scans, yet they flowed from my fingers to the screen. All pain I needed to endure again for my son. I read and studied the craft, then wrote and wrote some more. Still, I struggled, words meant for the trash, sentences not worthy of Strayed or Maclean, most of all, not deserving of my son.

I felt like my father probably had. He worked on his play for twenty years, never finishing it other than having a scene read in a small theater. I realized why that play meant so much to him, why he called everyone he knew and wore a sports jacket for the first time in years. He lived for those hours when he sat in front of his Olivetti typewriter, a highball glass sweating on his left, and a smoldering cigarette on his right. Pain billowing in the smoke as it floated to the ceiling. Had he and Dylan Thomas used those hours at La Stella or The White Horse to numb the torture of the word that wouldn't come, the sentence that wouldn't be, the story never read?

Still, I read and wrote, and a year later, I found a low-residency MFA program where I could focus on my writing. I took a week off and drove to Newport, RI. I returned to school at 53, with funds from Justin's 529 plan. During my first residency, I marveled at poets. Major Jackson, who slapped his hand on the podium, like he was Kanye West. Charles Coe who wrote poems named "Bowling with the Pope" and "Picnic on the Moon." I would not have been surprised if Charles had done those things. A half century after my parents named me, poets were suddenly hip, like baseball players were before they bought Ferraris and refused to sign autographs. But none was cooler than Edgar Kunz, who wore sneaker brands I'd never heard of, and formed his hair in a wavy, controlled mess. He wrote about his father's last days in a ramshackle house, poems that were gritty and approachable. He recited Dylan Thomas's "Do not go gentle into that good night," and then he paused, said, "Wow," pausing again for full effect. It sucked the air out of me. The rhythm of the words caught in my chest, not yet knowing what the poem meant.

Late that night, I set out to learn everything about Dylan Thomas. I scrutinized the pictures, studied the eyes of the man who wrote that poem, drank too much, let it all slip away. I returned again and again to one photo. One that reminded me of a picture of my father with a cigarette dangling from his mouth. Both men posed like James Dean, pores in their faces open, creases that held pain, photos meant for black and white. They were images from a time before the sharpness dulled in their eyes, before my father's hair grayed and receded, and before Thomas's face became bloated and weathered. Times in their lives before they longed for the next word and the bars that aged them both. I had never known those times or that father.

Laptop casting a blue hue on my face, I read "Do not go gentle into that good night" for the first time. I pieced it together like a movie I'd never seen in its entirety. I picked it apart, word by word, line by line, discovering it was a deeply personal poem about fathers and sons, living and dying. Perhaps, in writing, I found what my father and even Dylan Thomas could not. Both wanted to be writers, be artistic, had a disdain for anything else. I never thought of writing, but it became a welcome respite from the next glass of wine and the next day without my son.

Sometimes, when a plane strikes a building or a healthy child gets cancer, we try to explain what maybe can't be explained. Often, we don't understand those close to us and never will. A name, bar, and poem, in perfect sequence, required to understand a man who lived in New York but didn't like baseball. A man who wanted a different life for his son, just as I had for mine. I gave my all to save my son's body and soul, and possibly my father had struggled not to lose my soul, too. Maybe that weighed on him, as his body failed, and he waged a battle he did not know or care to fight.

My name, my father.

My darkest teacher, my poet.

His struggles, now my struggles.

His son, now my son.

For him, I write into the night ⬥

Look Inside a Woman for the World

by Christine Kalafus

When Connecticut shuts down, so does my uterus. "Aah, you have pandemic period," my OB-GYN says; I think about punctuation while her hand is inside me. Her first name ends in a soft *a*, like *massage*, like *adore*—like *ally*.

My first OB-GYN had a last name that ended in a *y*, like a question, so he should have been able to listen. As if his name wasn't a trick, as if his name was a soothing *why*, as if his name didn't shout *he*. His misdiagnosis should have resulted in my death. "That's not cancer, that's a clogged milk duct." As if the body could not build twins and also try to demolish the mother.

"My period took off on vacation," I tell Elena. She laughs and jokes back while her finger circles my cervix. "Where did it go?" she asks, paying attention. To myself, I answer, *I hid it like treasure, like gold, like toilet paper, like yeast—flour.* But to her I say, "Down to Savannah, on the vacation my husband and I booked but had to cancel. No one told my period. She's been gone for months."

In a preteen memory of my mother, she chooses sanitary pads from a grocery store shelf. The box is illustrated with a painting of a woman wearing a baby doll dress, skipping at the edge of the ocean like no woman in history wearing a giant wad between her legs, even if it is labeled Stayfree. As if being a woman has ever been free.

At the height of the pandemic, there are plenty of tampons: super plus, super, and regular. For some reason, there are no options with super plus and regular in the same box. If I was super plus for seven days, I'd be in the hospital—a word that contains *spit* so no wonder no one wants to be there. I hold in my abdomen, I leave without buying. As if I am storing up the blood so I won't need a transfusion if or when the time comes. As if I am storing up the blood to donate to my children, the state, the entire world.

At the end of June, the moment Connecticut's governor, who has a last name ending in a *t* like the tents he had set up in Hartford hospital parking lots, says, "Restrictions are being lifted, gently," I will be in the city's Elizabeth Park, in the middle of the rosebuds, bleeding right through my pants, oblivious, under the arbors, taking selfies—blooming. Returning to my car, I will find that I am saturated to my thighs. Turning the key, the gas gauge reads hard *e* like *female*, like *scream*, like *money*.

I'll wrap myself in the towel I use to protect the car's upholstery from my dog's wet body after hikes by the stream, pumping gas with my lower half covered in a print of mama and baby goldfish.

On store shelves, there is Charmin, Fleischmann's, and King Arthur, neatly restocked after the shortage. Everyone in the grocery is calm, in straight lines, properly masked, six feet apart—while my body spirals down into cramps. I will place two boxes of the dwindling supply of tampons in my cart when what I want to do is load box after box after box into my arms, catapult over the checkout, and steal out the store's sliding doors.

But that is next month. Right now, Elena palpates, navigates. I'm leaning back like I just mowed the lawn, enjoying a nap in a hammock, but I'm busy writing inside my rawness, memorizing this moment of being heard. She's reading me like my uterus is braille. A word that focuses on feeling—a word that ends with a listening *e*, like the one at the end of her last name, like the one at the end of my first, like the one at the end of *circle*, like the one at the beginning of *earth*.

The Archaeology of Memory, Part II: The (Re)-Creation of the Self

by Jason Courtmanche

I knew a girl in college named Green, a wonderful painter and beautiful. Her paintings were abstract, full of colors and shapes like a Kandinsky but with softer, fuller lines. She used to destroy most of her work before anyone saw it. I fantasized about sleeping with her. I wanted her to paint something for me so incomplete in its ability to convey the emotions of our intimacy that she destroyed it at once.

I knew a boy at UConn who grew up in Mansfield. I've forgotten his name. He went to school with us, but as a hometown boy he lived with his mother. We called him late one night to invite ourselves to his home. We were fascinated by him. He was solitary, unknowable. There were wondrous depths to him we wanted to explore. His mother answered our call. She was friendly but reluctant to invite us over. He, too, was hesitant on the phone. He warned us his room was small, an attic. When we arrived, we were ushered into a close-ceilinged space filled everywhere with piles of books and magazines, and boxes full of rocks and shells and feathers. It was as if he had never in his life discarded anything, and his old mother, out of love and desperate acceptance, had consigned him and his awful accumulation of life's things to her attic. I thought of T.S. Eliot shoring up fragments against the ruins.

As an undergraduate I would smoke pot in the grey mornings of winter before walking to class across the old part of UConn, through the early morning fog that rolled off the lake and past the bare trees, and across the open field that today has sidewalk and lights. I loved the old brick buildings and the towering oak and the pine trees. It was easy to lose myself in time and imagine I were walking across campus in the previous century. I would experience an odd nostalgia for the present, as writer Paul Auster calls it, that enabled me to appreciate the present moment more by looking at it as if it were the past—as if the very moment I lived in was a memory, and I could be comforted the way only memory can: by the familiarity of the scene.

Years later, after I had a son and my father had disappeared, I would experience a different kind of nostalgia in which I would see my childhood self in my son and wanted to weep for the boy I was—lonely, almost fatherless, and peripatetic. When my son became old enough, he would ask me while lying in bed at night to tell him stories of my childhood, and I realized that most of my memories were sad or from my teens and twenties when I lived an outrageous life that strove to banish the memories of my sadness and anger. But I could not tell those stories to him yet. Instead, I offered him the handful of happy memories I had—of eating a hot dog with my father outside the Peabody Museum, of seeing a fish jump out of Lake Whitney as my father and I rode our bikes across the causeway, of ice-skating on Holland Pond near my grandparents' cottage.

For years my wife and I have taken in strays: high school and college students, children left afloat as we had been by absent parents and difficult circumstance. Over the years, the web of our intimate relationships grew. The notion of family, of what it means to love or be in love, expanded and defined by empathy rather than blood.

Many years ago, we were invited to the first wedding of a former student. I was asked to stand in for her father and give a reading at the ceremony and a toast at the reception. We have been to the weddings of several other students since then, all our former strays. Relationship after relationship, I find myself inserted into the fatherless lives of these students and acting the part of the father I never really had. After almost thirty years of teaching, I have watched them become adults, marry, and begin their careers—many choosing to teach English like me. In just this past year, one had a baby. Another has begun law school. A third is trying to recreate her life from the ashes of her failed marriage. A fourth confronts the likelihood that she will have to do the same. These former students, now friends, meet me for coffee, a drink. Some write to me late at night seeking advice or just a friendly voice. As Hemingway writes, "It is awfully easy to be hard-boiled about everything in the daytime, but at night it is another thing."

I seek solace in a late-night glass of wine and a book in the woods around my house, in the things that grow in the gardens of my yard. Do the demons ever leave, or do they merely recede? I remind myself that our fate is only the story we craft. "Death is the mother of beauty," said Wallace Stevens. Daily, I resurrect memory, crafting identity by choosing what to suppress and what to preserve.

Birds

by Kethry Bentz

Blue and green parakeets you named and unnamed and named in a squall of lost monikers perched on the bars of their cage on Pfeffer Lane. Budgies who crooned, who mewled, who sang back your nightmares and grieved by your husband's chair on those nights his voice pushed through the stone at Saint Peter Cemetery and sent you wandering. Your blinds stayed shut when the sun was high, when the breeze was warm, when the wild birds sang beyond your locked windows. Bolted and locked up tight in the tub, you hide in the shadows of your shower curtain from the phantom men and their phantom flashlights outside. Your mind showed you what wasn't there; my mind adjusted to the state of yours. Behind the door, beyond the walls, past the window of your car that's rolled down, all the way down, we drive the back roads, hunting for yard sales, and you smile with round cheeks and ask in soft words, "Are you cold?" but I'm too shy to say yes.

Illuminated beneath the light of God, I wonder if you still would have liked me as I am today. Inheritances of dolls and jewelry that I never knew existed and don't know what to do with tell me that although you once loved me, you never knew me. When I favored Hot Wheels and faded baseball gloves, you always thought nail paint and antique brass earrings would make me happy. And instantly, I'm moved, because I picture your knobby fingers scrawling one of my names, the only one you knew, and I know you remembered me asleep in the crib in your basement. I invent a life for you, stare into the pool in your backyard, and hear your words sink and settle on the broken liner.

I invite your lost memories and the fears you kept hidden in the bathtub from the phantom men.

I look in the mirror and I see your cheeks.

Reality and delusion look the same through moldy windows. Remaining inside was the only answer that questioned your stability. Running water to fill the tub, hoping the steam would grow in time to stretch and reach across the glass, veiling your soft words and my round cheeks and the weeping willow outside. Results were found in shrouding the windows, hiding away from lights that weren't there, and swallowing pills to stop your shaking fingers. Refreshed and relieved you were alone once more, you tried to leave the bathroom, but the handle wouldn't turn and their flashlights rested on the back of my neck, which you kissed because I faked sick again to get out of school.

Relapse because I forgot my pills after your funeral service at St. Peter, so I put them in my mouth with shaking fingers and gaze out the glass at the willow.

Do angels sing for those they cursed? Delight in the time we shared, now twisted and warped beneath the weight of failing memories. Detach from the inherited fears, biological dread, the delusions and paranoia that filled your heart with panic and now creep toward mine. Dementia creased the lines of your face and you squeezed my cheeks with both hands and kissed me. Doughnuts and Fig Newtons were hidden in the lower cabinets, next to the tiny boxes of cereal I ate by the pool and got soggy. Divine icons and emblems on your walls and on your tables that normally scared me in churches only felt inviting and warm, not like I was hiding my secrets but like they knew my secrets and didn't mind. Remembering the days I didn't want to see you and hearing my dad tell me I would regret it. I pretend I got in his car with him and drove to your house anyway, where your unnamed budgies greeted me from their cage. I develop a means to forgive myself, to remind myself we are all unnamed to one another.

Sweet and jubilant, I hear your laugh as they place your ashes into the ground. Sunshine is veiled behind afternoon clouds and I stand between uncomfortable and uncertain uncles and cousins who throw dirt on you and hide their red eyes. Sacred words for a religion that no one here understands are uttered at the dirt before your gruff sons try to convince the nervous teenage gravedigger to let them reposition one of the sinking headstones. Soothing songs from the trees above rain down on us from the beaks of the uncaged, the unnamed. Staring at the fresh earth covering you, I wonder how many times you stared out from the bathroom at the willow in your yard, how many times I will do the same. Spirits live in this family graveyard in southeastern Massachusetts, but for once in my life, I am not afraid of ghosts nor men outside windows.

Standing beside you in the bathroom, I remind myself to open the blinds.

POETRY

LAZYBONES BLUES

by Margaret Gibson

Let's spend the day in bed, all day in bed,
at least until noon, and without so much
as a stitch on. Let's offer
the eager advocates of meritocracy
a way smack out the door. May they
leave quietly and not disturb our rest.
And let's never say, "We deserve this."
Even to think it, risks getting us back,
climbing the Himalayas of accomplishment—
hurried, harried, heart-worn,
and breathing the thin air of peaks and pinnacles.
Back in a time of angst and ambition,
a friend said, "You look like a starving
Aphrodite." But now we can picnic
on bedsheets redolent with the scent
of our bodies, now doze in a summer's
hum of bees as they do their fervent
renditions of the blues, now savor
the honey that drips from the lip
of each moment, recovering from losses
we didn't even know we had. If life is
a brief parenthesis, let's pull the sheets up
over our heads, and with our bodies
pressed together side by side, your arms
around me, my long thigh slung over your hip,
let's take our ease. Let's not bring even one

book to bed. Let's bless every misuse of
lie and *lay*. Let's lay down all day. Let's vow
to be perfectly useless. I've laid by
a store of mangoes and roses. Make a wish.
Mine is to forget everything except
what happens after (oh yes) you kiss my breasts.

Indigo Insomnia

by Monica Ong

Indigo insomnia is a shrine of candles on the street corner of sudden absence, their dying strewn with flowers and handmade signs. Sleep, a scraggly stray, breathes with its tongue hanging low, sniffing each offering of dolls dampened by rain. Pauses. Then scurries into the alley towards the other side of amnesia.

Mother never told me my auntie's name was Juanita until she was near death, dying, or long dead. I can't remember. I called her by her title, Ah-Ching: as in Mother's Eldest Sister, as in Hidden Hurt, as in First Fire & Last Ember, as in Silent Shame Waiting Behind the Trees. We say the names of the dead more often in afterlife than during the departed's lifetime.

Indigo insomnia is the great waking, this birthing of the world anew. *From the indigo, an even deeper blue*, it is said.[1] Perhaps this is why father hardly slept my entire childhood. His thin frame disappearing into the long white lab coat. A square photo of my face in one pocket, and a black pager in the other, both blinking as he walked his rounds until the gray-blue dawn.

The mouth holds many things except the language of the new, still forming between the lungs. The spoken vow we breathe, but don't yet know how to defend. Scrolling through the phone, one sees mostly ghosts or the self, ghosted, an accounting of

1 From the classical Chinese work *Hsün Tzu* (*Great Concentration and Insight*) T'ien-t'ai, 594, often cited by Nichiren Daishonin (*Writings of Nichiren Daishonin*, p. 457.)

strings stretched and broken. Someone slightly out of tune. Wondering if your voice is in the wrong chord, the wrong song, the wrong language, or just a painting of the ocean, its roar muted by a gilded gaze that sees but doesn't listen.

Indigo insomnia is diving into the deepest waters of memory to uncover the bodies hidden by our bad inheritance. My anxious study of patterns and vertices that squint for a brand-new design. It is to know that there are no saviors except for that one decision standing outside your screen door. During the pandemic, brown paper packages pile up on the front porch like an avalanche of grievances. Time slows down so we can notice. Every person I pass on the street walks with an abandoned child clinging onto their backs. I look into those round, wet eyes and my mouth feels the same hunger, dry and gritty with ocean salt.

The problem with numbers that count our deaths is that they don't carry the smell of moss or fresh-cut grass from the bottom of your brother's shoes. They easily forget that one is sometimes two, that bitter melons are actually sweet if you eat them far from home. You cannot hear the hours of static nor the quiet breathing of your mother swirling in clouds of dirty rice water between the long, wet grains and your cold fingertips moving in circles. This is why it is called *lossy* data.

Indigo insomnia is the truth asking for a ring in her latest ultimatum. It is stillness acknowledging the injuries painted over by the flag or a blight of bronze. The mass grave of bodies that rise beneath Christmas snow year after year. Their cause of death and elaborate cover-up, one in the same. In school we call it History, enshrine terror in red, white, and blue ribbons that we wear in our permed hair to match summer's twirling dresses. Orchestrated fires pop across the black body of July's night sky. Children gather to lick patriotic popsicles named after the bomb. ⬟

The Arrogances

by Benjamin S. Grossberg

I had the arrogance of takes no pills.
I had all the arrogances. The arrogance
of waiting for better. Of refusing
to explain. Of no gray in my beard
after forty and none on my chest,
which I flaunted on various apps.
I do not mention the arrogance of
regular dentistry and a reliable car.
But I had those, too. I never had that
of height or I-can-beat-you-up, useful
both for erotic and commercial
applications, but I still found ways
to get along, mostly by staying in corners
and wearing boots. Death's arrogance
flummoxed me, its supercilious refusal
of even the most supplicant address.
My mother, for example, when my father
drives up to her grave, conveniently
located at the end of a row. Does

the nearby tree explain her hauteur?
Not every plot has one. In winter,
he parks beneath it, engine on, heat
going, staying as long as he can take it.
My arrogance on the phone as he
tells me this manifests in platitudes.
I won't get started on the arrogance
of platitudes. Enough to say that I
was full of it—like stones in my pocket,
weighing me into a lake. But other
arrogances buoyed me. Especially
looks-good-for-his-age, which,
in my arrogance, I took as an insult.
Also hope-as-expectation, and saying
hell no to the obvious. But pills every
morning should have been my first clue.
And increasing blotchiness of face.
And that rafter of men not texting back.
One by one, the departing arrogances:
little ballerinas twirling offstage, each
in her puffed-out skirt. The arrogance
of consciousness may well be last to go,
the final ballerina, pirouetting away.
And look, her slipper's come loose! ◈

Dear Future Daughter

by Nora Holmes

Dear Future Daughter,

I'm writing in case we never meet—in case this virus reaches me before you do. The more the cases rise, the more I think about you and try to reach out for another person I cannot touch.

I picture your hands gripped around a Ticonderoga pencil as you're filling out an assignment for your elementary school history class. It will be the assignment where you have to interview an older generation on something Important that happened in their lifetime. And I imagine your hair will be tawny brown like mine is, and maybe you'll have one of those grippies around your pencil; the one you begged me to buy for you in the checkout line at Staples. And you'll ask me what it was like in 2020, and what it felt like to be alive when the world was dying.

I will tell you about the silence. How the air was still, the streets were empty, and the parking lots had been reclaimed by the crows.

I will tell you it was hidden in the little things, all this dying. I saw it in the grimly headlined papers thrown at the end of our driveway by the weary driver of a weathered Toyota, but I also saw it as one, then two, then three ambulances passed me on my morning run. I saw it in the eyes of the people I passed, the way they looked down and held their breaths when they saw me.

We were all choking on our own resistance to death. Some of us craved life enough to hide from it behind locked doors and windows and cloths tied behind our ears.

And if you ask again later, when you are older, I will tell you more.

The week of the protests, the demands for life to be sacred again. The hope chanted through all of us into the megaphones of the young, Black, Womxn activists, and how they too met tear gas and rubber bullets.

I will explain to you that the government left us to die. How they promised money and supplies and relief that never came. And I will tell you about all the times Politics with a capital P came up, and how many times I heard it said that No One Is Coming To Save Us. And I will protect you from hope, which never came either.

Hurricane Isaias came, and took out our light. The branches fell and locked us into our block, isolating us three times over. They charged us more for the power than they ever had before and then left us in the dark. It took them days to give the light back and clear away the bodies of the trees that used to shelter us.

And the people who used to shelter us, we lost them too. There was a beautiful girl with copper colored hair I saw every day on the way to my first period class. I missed her in the spring, I missed the feeling of other people pushing me along through the hallway, knowing I could not fall if they were there holding me up. I longed for the way it felt as someone's hand brushed against my skin.

I will want to start crying in front of you, weeping, sobbing for everything that was lost that year. The silence and the flames and the wind and the touch, all of it will still be there under my skin, waiting to come cascading out.

In June, I went to an aviary. I saw beautiful feathers stuck in the wires of the fences, and talons that could have sliced the pale skin of my hands if I tried to get too close. It was haunting, all this feral beauty.

I've spent more time than I used to watching the birds in the yard as they preen in puddles and raise chicks under my window. And I think that when you come,

when I reach you,

I will call you Wren.
My Little Bird.

And your feathers will not be electric and your song will not pierce the morning, but it will still make me weep when I hear it.

You will not be displayed for the world to see and touch and adore.

But you will live.
You will survive.
You will endure.

In the Time of Sonic Booms

by B. Fulton Jennes

Maybe we were running toward trees
across a field strewn with sunlight;
maybe we were worming through
culverts, digging a dog's grave,
biking with no hands on the grips;

maybe we were watching the flight
of a baseball, a bird, a father's hand;
maybe we saw the steely glint in the sky

before our chests became hollow drums
struck by sound louder than sound,
sound that was fist, bat, bludgeon,
sound felt more than heard.

Maybe it was more than a hole ripped
in sky by a machine practicing menace,
learning to drop bombs dumbly
like a deer that shits while it walks;

maybe it was us, just us, imagining
a god even angrier than the one
who once hung his own son on a tree,
who was eager now to show us his face,
who knew exactly where we lived.

AT INNISFREE GARDEN

by Bessy Reyna

In the pond the geese chase the heron
as if demanding—*get away from us!*
you are too beautiful!

The heron stands alone
in the middle of the mucky water
observing his surroundings, turning
the long periscope that is his neck

away from him
geese congregate like noisy children at recess.
Four of them follow one another
in perfect formation
resembling early morning scull rowers
training on the river.

The heron hasn't moved.

Bessy Reyna

Echoes of people talking in the distance
reverberate and a playful child runs and
throws a stone in the water
making it ripple, expand
reaching the heron.

A family, speaking a language
I do not know,
walks behind me.

All over the park
the yearly transformation to
yellows and oranges
compels us to surrender to its beauty,
while red leaves cover the ground
like autumn's blood. ❧

Demeter's Other Children

by Sean Frederick Forbes

Did the steady flow of flaxen summer honey
from the thyrsus of Dionysus slow to a coveted

trickle? Did iridescent slivers of beeswax, once swallowed,
offer the slim possibility of celestial insight?

Did Arion develop an extraordinary gallop, hooves
stomping a rhythmic reminder to frozen soil

that spring would come again as he hummed
a tune no one could decipher? Did Plutus pivot

decisions on how to dispense gifts of wealth
due to his sister's yearly disappearance—more

havoc than necessary? Did Philomelus pace anxiously,
the initial shock of fallen leaves, his lost

industriousness too cruel as his mighty oxen
and venerable plow took rest? Did Despoina,

the other daughter, despair in becoming the lady
of the house to a brood of brothers and a distressed

mother? Did they assure themselves the promise made
with Hades was a sacred pact, that the underworld

house of Persephone would always be transitory? 🛡️

Some Questions You Might Ask about the Universe

by Christine Beck

How many football fields, jelly beans, motes of stardust
to get from here, right here, to there—

to the crisp edge of the universe, burned
like cookies on a metal tray. And where is there?

Do astrophysicists know something they aren't saying?

Do they show up daily at the lab, shrug on their official
white coats, power up the cyclotron, then step outside

for a coffee, bask on sunny steps like salamanders,
run their fingers through their trusty spaniel's fur,

having concluded that the question is unsolvable?
Or maybe the solution is too terrible to contemplate.

Maybe they have found the edge. Maybe they have proved
the ancients were correct: the world is as flat as Kansas.

Maybe they have peered into a roiling pit, like a slash
of dark from childhood closets left ajar,

a void choked up with Coke cans, Walmart bags,
plastic straws, and a universe of dirty diapers.

Maybe they already know there is no coffee there,
no sunshine, and definitely no spaniels. 🏵

Sweet Spot

by David Cappella

It could've been the music
in his brain that summoned
the urge to push himself up
to sit at the edge of the bed.
It could've been a memory
of his old, favored Martin
that he played every day
even when swordfishing
out on Georges Bank.
Perhaps the myeloma decided
to give his marrow a break.

"Tryin' to find my sweet spot,"
he mumbled, groggy, caught
between reclining and sitting up,
wrestling with pain in a search
for the comfort of equilibrium.

David Cappella

Face palsied from glomus
tumors, cotton mouthed,
clouded eyes, drug-lidded—
all that doughy loose flesh.

Strange, this abrupt sitting up,
oblivious to me, to the disease.
Stranger still, the sudden gesture—
he began to air play a guitar
with hands so nimble, so precise.

The left slid along the neck,
lingered over imagined frets,
fingers mimicked chords:
A E F#M A7/g D Dm;
the right pantomimed rhythmic
strums on invisible strings:
down, down up, down, down up.

His flabby body swayed
to the silent song he heard
but had no strength to sing,
enraptured by the uncanny,
by an unbidden sweet spot.

Then, just like that, he stopped,
crumpled back onto the hospital bed,
his body a slow-motion writhe
of twists and turns—a deflated balloon:
my younger brother two days
before his heart gives out.

I Say Pick a Side

by Z'Jahniry Coleman

"Females are too sensitive," they say.
"Females know how to keep it real," they say.
"Females talk a lot," they say.
But then again . . .
"Females are too aggressive," they say.
"Females are fake," they say.
"Females are too quiet," they say.
It never ends.
Pick a side, I say.
Pick a side.

There are too many rules for us to abide.
Anything we do or say is always taken in the wrong way.
Anything we say or do is always a problem in the world's view.
We fix our hair, we fix our clothes,
we paint our fingers and our toes,
some even contour their nose
but still don't reach the standard.

Some put on makeup
after a breakup
or just to dress up,
impress up.
But then we are hiding our natural face,
right?
Rated one out of ten,
lowering our confidence and then
we are labeled by these crazy things we call men.

You can't wear too much makeup.
But then again . . .
You can't leave the house without it.
No joy.
You can't show too much skin or wear clothes that are too tight.
But then again . . .
You can't be fully covered or you'll look like a boy.
Pick a side, I say.
Pick a side.

The world is male dominated,
females hated, rated, weighted.
Females have to achieve something to be respected.
Why can't we support each other and be a collective?
It's hard enough being a female,
not to mention a Black one.
Let's try to support one another
and be united as one.

Stereotype.

A word that isn't worth all the hype.

Some may be false, some may be true,

but everything is different in someone else's shoes,

so try looking through our point of view.

Pick a side, I say.

Pick a side.

Professional Harpist

by Julie Choffel

is what my mom was.
This is what I told my music class
in a lesson on instruments
when I was very little.

My mother was a PE teacher.
Of course, it was me
who lusted after ethereal & moody vibrations
just like it was me who would never do a single pull-up
or hit it out of the park. Who even

needed tangible ambitions
when you could be anything at all: this
was the lesson of the harp. Larger than the body
playing it, embracing it, ridiculously shaped
like a wobbly portal
or the mouth of a whale. Noise
unlike noise, noise that carried a body

almost away. *Oh, really!*
my teacher must have said
in the usual way of those who know
how to protect the wide-eyed
from the profane. *Yeah, really,*
I may have replied, rapt
by my own vision, my mom following
her harp around the world, *it's incredible.*

Inheritance

by Kelly de la Rocha

from my mother's father:
a cardboard box full of opaque
film containers

                cradling

desiccated garden seeds –
canisters labeled with grease pencil
in his shaky hand:
Italian parsley,
Ma's-Myra hybrid tomatoes,
marigolds, 1997 –

                his legacy of

long-gone growing seasons –
omitted from his will,
just like me.

He would have preferred
these

                     carefully culled
                     kernels
                     of creation

claimed by one of his own
gender.
Instead they sat abandoned
beneath the greenhouse planting table
where they found me

                     overflowing
                     with beginnings,
                     rattling with spring.

Scenes from an Italian American Bridal Shower

by Kenneth DiMaggio

"Even if it's not your first time,
let the man think it is."

"Lorraine, whattiya telling the poor girl!"

"Nuttin' you didn't tell me before my
bridal shower!"

"Okay, girls, let Lisa open her presents,"
a wise old aunt announces.

Oohing and ahhing
as a young bride-to-be
holds up a glass mason jar
sprouting artificial sunflowers.

"They're supposed to be dandy-
lions," explains a Lucia or Maria.

Kenneth DiMaggio

Ooh ooh ooh
as the soon-to-be wedded
holds up a large fork and spoon
that are wooden.

"Good for cookin' and also
disciplinin' the kids once
they start walking."

"Aww, don't spoil her fun!"
warns a wise new mother who
then advises:

"And have it as long as you
can before you have kids."

Mm-hmm mm-hmm
mm-hmm

nods a roomful of wise
married women.

I Want That, Let Me Get It (Love, Peace, and Joy)

by Brittany Walls

There's no problem
With asking for what you want
The vitalities of life
Is what I need right now
To make me whole
Love, peace, and joy
I want them, let me get it
I want this here love
I want that old-school kind of love
90s R&B men ballads,
In the car singing my heart out kind of love
Traveling After 7 to H-Town
Making room every night
For this kind of love
Midnight, late in my feelings,
Dreaming of you kind of love
Drowning in my floor
Swirling in lyrics of Marvin

Kind of love
The Michael Jackson
Lady of my life verse number 2
Kind of love
The "you're the one for me"
Because "I believe in you and me"
Whitney always loving you
Kind of love
The Coltrane to your
Love Supreme kind of love
That's all I want
I want peace and tranquility
I want that head to my pillow,

Pitch black, no alarm clock needed
Kind of peace
The trailing in the wilderness,
I dare you come find me
Kind of peace
The down South, willow trees
Humming just for me
In the breeze kind of peace
The sparks flying off my pen
Because my paper is lit
Kind of peace
The bills paid, doors locked,
Everybody leave me alone
Kind of peace
The "I'd rather talk to my book friends
Than you" kind of peace

That's all I want
I want that joy
That sounds of blackness "joy"
Kind of joy
The after-school, act like I have
No homework, playing outside
With dem kids down the street
Kind of joy
The "I wear my natural hair,
Whatchu gon say about it?"
Fresh off those flexi rods
Kind of joy
The "I made this, and you bought it"
First sale kind of joy
The canceled plans I didn't want
To go to in the first place,
Introvert vibes kind of joy
The "found one hundred dollars in front of Walmart
After I didn't have enough money
In the store" kind of joy

The "I left food in the 'frigerator,
It better be there" and it is kind of joy
The waking up to self-care day
All day long kind of joy
The covers over my head,
Watching Spike Lee movies
Because I see myself in them
Kind of joy
The wrapped in my mother's arms,

Brittany Walls

Joyous she is still here kind of joy
That's all I want
Is that too much to ask for?

Daughter Sic Transit

by James Finnegan

Walking to the bus station, I have a guitar case
in my hand. I could be an aging rocker afraid
to leave the road, on his way to another small city gig.
In fact I'm carrying my daughter's guitar.
I may be a frequent flier, but she's gotta be
Platinum Plus on Greyhound by now.
Many times I have heard her called someone
who is finding her way, a free spirit, which is to say,
one who is windblown, of no certain address.
A couch surf in any odd apartment, sleeping
rough under sumac by the overpass, what does
she care? And my worry won't keep her safe,
so let this be a prayer: When I hear what is only leaves
scuffing up the driveway, I'll think it's her.

Little Women by Louisa May Alcott

by Cathy Fiorello

I always prayed I'd dream of *Little Women*,
the book that bore me through childhood.
Meg, Jo, Beth, and Amy—
I'd be the fifth sister, the desperate one
who flirted and drank champagne.

Just once, they did come to me in a dream:
but they traipsed about their Civil War winter
as if I weren't there,
as if I hadn't given them my best days and nights
learning by heart their joys, their woes,
sacrificing real friendships for their company.

They ignored me like everyone else.

So, I grew more flamboyant,
smoking behind the school at twelve,
failing classes with wicked panache,
attempting suicide,

wearing capes, blue-tinted glasses,
holding up McDonald's with a lighter that looked like a gun,
becoming an atheist.

Still, no one saw.

Despite their indifference,
each night I'd return to the March family,
where Father was at war,
and the girls brought Christmas dinner to the poor.

When they sang hymns around the piano,
I would sit in the corner,
the ghost of Christmas future,
sharpening my stiletto and hoping for the best.

The Pages Are So Beautiful, We Touch Them Twice

by Amy L. Nocton

Dedicated to my father who captured some of these words from *Love Lies Bleeding* Don Delillo, 2005 in his diary years before he died from early onset Alzheimer's in November 2019

When the sky has lost more buttons
and basil scents the summer air,
we will remember the snow on a Portland street in August

and its models cloaked in winter whites,
a haunting holiday recollection
unexpected.

In the end it's not what kind of man he was, but simply
that he's gone. The stark
fact.

Snow fell once in August on a Maine street. While, in another
state, our father slept a forgotten hospice slumber blanketed
in cold, conditioned air white.

Amy L. Nocton

The highway overpass's
arrows had shown us the way
All points to Maine

as we navigated
the unfamiliar narrow
dark.

Later, after his passage, the pages
are so beautiful, we touch
them twice

work over the air
held by each word, each pause,
each breath

contained in his diary,
or in the dog-eared
books

where we magnify, still,
the magnificent, where
love lies bleeding.

Rituals

by Victoria Nordlund

I wake up at 5:05 a.m. to pick my poodle's eyes open.

Lift her off the couch to pee outside.

It is twelve degrees and she eats the snow. It must feel good in her old throat.

I stand without socks at the sliding door guiding her up an Astroturfed ramp.

She eats four tins of Cesar Beef Recipe dog food and waits to be carried down

to my mom's green pull-out couch in the basement.

I cover her with a teal comforter,

tell her to have a good day at work.

(She no longer asks to be petted but I do this part anyway.)

I go upstairs to have my K-cup coffee.

Pour my Starbucks caramel creamer into the glass mug everyone knows not to take.

Drink it in the dark at the kitchen table.

My mom's birthday is next week.

For a few years after she died I went to the Paper Store

and stood for way too long in the card aisle selecting the right one.

I used to call her every morning at 6:15 on my commute.

I have her flip phone in my purse.

Her pocketbook is next to my nightstand.

She would have been ninety-two.

I have the peppermint oil I bought her in bulk on Amazon the day before she died.

Apply it to my wrists now and then.

We would go to Burtons for a birthday martini. She liked hers dirty. Relished the olives.

We would sit at the round table by the front.

I would help her walk, then walker, then wheelchair

over to Chico's to buy some black blouses.

The same saleslady would greet us and ask how we were doing and

I wonder if she is still there.

It is still dark when I start my car.

Clear just enough frost off to make it

until the heat kicks in.

I always come back to the same playlist now,

Continuum timed perfectly for each traffic light.

One, two, one-two-three—

Matryoshka Doll

by Lorraine Riess

Is it mother to mother
to mother or
daughter to daughter
to daughter?
Each quaint peasant
brightly painted and bulbous,
expectant for generations

down to the smallest nugget
offered up by the sacrifice
of those hollowed out halves.
No belly to pry open
with predictable delight,
she stands silent among her forebears.

I pick up this last little one
and see myself in her
as the end of our maternal line.
The dark wood knot
that shows through the paint,
a swirl of contrarian inclinations.

I didn't intend to be selfish
just wary of the hardships
I saw in the women around me
who took grandkids as the final prize
as if commensurate with their efforts.

My mother never asked and I never offered
to explain why I chose no children.
Perhaps she feared it may have been
some fault of hers she didn't want to hear.

How self-contained these dolls remain
as I piece them back together.
This last little one with her similar smile
has fended off the carver
who would have whittled one more of us.

Love Letter from the House Plant to the Tea Kettle

by Samantha Schwind

They told me
I was meant for a life in the shade,
a seat by the clearest window, and that you
would just hang me up
to leave me high and dry.

They said
I was too young, far too
green for love, and that you
would just burn up
the seeds of my blossoming
potential.

They told me
I would always be turning toward
your chromium charm just to hear you whistle
after some porcelain model, and that you
were filled with far too much

hot air
for someone as
calm, cool, and collected
as me.
They told me
that you were nothing more
than a dream,
insubstantial as steam.

But I
know you,
I've seen you, and I
have a feeling deep
in my roots about you.

I have seen past
your shiny, stainless-steel armor,
and I have felt
your calm inner warmth.

I will let you make tea
and cool down with me
in peace
whenever you please.

If loving you
means getting steamy, bring on
the fire, I will leave this windowsill behind
in pursuit of desire. I'm accustomed
to weekly waterings, but with you, I'll take
whatever you're willing to give.

And I know
we live in different worlds,
and we're both always
really busy,
but in my dreams,
when we face each other,
it is so bright that I
always
wake up feeling like
sunlight—so
maybe one day, you'll
leave your fiery hot spot to come
join me by the window

and when the rosy glow of dawn
casts shadows behind us and
promise ahead, we will turn
to face each other in the light
of the new world, and my reflection
will be, always, you.

Reflections on a Closed Border

by Wendy Tarry

Somedays the border
is a slash of lipstick on a mirror:
a hard red stop line
leaving my looking glass
half emptied.

Somedays the border
is a finger-string,
soft-twine reminder
of what might yet be.

The familiar fold on the map
has become a locked door.
The hinge between
my homelands
snapped shut.

Wendy Tarry

I used to cross
the Thousand Islands Bridge
stomach lurching like
a roller-coaster rider,
the steep ascent of anticipation,
the hanging pause
of papers and questions,
and then
the welcome rush of home.
Now I stand
tokenless
at the empty turnstile
of waiting.

If the border was a river
I could wade in,
reeds whispering against my ankles,
launch leaf boats
to the other side,
send my mother a letter
on birchbark carefully peeled.

If the border was a stone wall
I could lean my back
on rock and moss
and know my father leaned
against the other side.

But since it is not those things
I will imagine
the border is
that little sliver of space
between two hands
as they reach for each other
an emptiness
at any moment to be crossed by love.

The Movie World

by Daniel Donaghy

There you are on the set, real dad of the girl whose movie dad,
the script says, is newly widowed and in town only for Christmas
until he runs into his high school flame. He's taller than you, younger,

Instagram famous, hair so perfect even the caterer finds reason
to touch it, his arms thick as thighs beneath cable-knit sweaters.
You heard someone say *a model, college football, The Bachelor.*

You note how little energy he burns compared to how much
he attracts: He stands stone-still between takes and playful questions
come from the crew in waves: *Dog person or cat person? Favorite emoji?*

He answers each with a rehearsed seriousness and a smile, speaking
softly as if into a boom mic, and with an unblinking gaze,
compels whoever's in front of him to enter for a moment a scene

the same for him whether cameras roll or not, a charged
exchange of laughter and awkward silence that the other person
always breaks first, like your daughter did in the hotel lobby

before he extended an elbow to her in these post-handshake times.
What really gets you is how kind he's been to her, twelve,
costumed in pigtails and sparkly pink boots to play ten, who,

in her excitement to be on a film set, to be anywhere free
for two weeks from remote learning, remote friends, is a running
faucet of giggles and small talk. She asks him his favorite color,

his middle name, makes him guess the names of her pets,
and he never once steps away, some part of her opening
here in Tulsa, Oklahoma, like the door to the flower shop

they'll walk through together in the next scene, hitting
their marks in front of the register to pay for the best tree
in the makeshift lot, a Fraser fir longer than their car

and wider, the one they'd picked a scene earlier while rare
lake-effect snow blew in off Oologah to the north, clumps of it
stuck to precise spots on their hats by the continuity director

before each slate clap, before movie dad, reaching for his wallet,
recognized in multiple takes from three different angles
the woman in the soiled smock as she dropped a box

of ornaments and the plot turned as predictably as a road
leading home, the dad's decision to stay in town, start over,
live near his sister and, of course, the shop owner, who falls

for your daughter because she, too, lost her mother as a girl,
the spontaneous hug they share sealing their scripted bond
in the scrim-soft light of a straight-to-TV movie world

you've clicked past each Christmas, never stopping
to consider art for which sweetness is the sole, simple point,
sweetness that will offer a salve for ninety minutes to soothe

these burning days if cable picks the film up, which the director
is confident it will, based on his contacts and experience,
based on the huge market for hope and happy endings

with fresh starts in towns never named, like the one
in which your daughter has gotten to shine for a while
while you held her coat behind the camera's eye.

FICTION

WHEN IT'S YOU

by Christopher Torockio

Wes Funderburke needs to shut up. Like now. He sits directly across the table from Angie, talking about the stock market, his face freshly shaved and splotchy pink, a Band-Aid on his bald dome where they recently scraped off what might yet turn out to be a cancerous mole. But it won't be. In the past two-and-a-half years, Wes Funderburke has had, from top to bottom, multiple melanomas, a double bypass with two stents, gallstones removed, blood clots clipped off in his legs, and surgery for severe Morton's neuroma in his foot. Yet here he is, having just devoured his osso buco and awaiting a slice of red velvet cake. He claims the cake is for him and his wife, Carol, to share. But Carol will sip her coffee, oblivious, while Wes eats the whole thing along with a shot of Sambuca. When the check is placed on the table, each couple will toss in some cash or a credit card, presumably splitting the bill four ways. But Angie didn't order dessert, and while everyone else ordered cocktails and bottles of wine, she didn't have anything to drink either. Just water. An appetizer as her entrée. No way she's spent twenty bucks in total. The three other couples are probably pushing a hundred each. She shouldn't have to "split" the bill. If Jim were still here, he'd handle it. She wouldn't know *how* much they've spent, and she wouldn't care, though she and Jim would talk and laugh about the silly injustice of it all on the drive home. You'd think someone would say, *Hey, the DePaolas didn't have any wine. Maybe they shouldn't have to pay as much.* Wouldn't you? But oh well, what were you gonna do? These were their friends; they'd known each other forever. Angie and Jim had always enjoyed their company and looked forward to their evenings out with them.

Now, though, no—Angie does not look forward to evenings out with these people. She feels bad about this fact, a little guilty, but everything is different now. She accepts their invitations because the dinners give her something to do, an excuse to get out of the house, an event to look forward to, words and times to scribble on her calendar because the alternative—being home after the sun goes down, just herself and the dog—is unbearable. Her running joke is, "Don't invite me to something just to be nice. Because I *will* accept." Everyone always laughs at this.

But seriously, why should she have to pay the same amount as the Funderburkes? She won't say anything, of course. She'll keep smiling, keep laughing, and then she'll be annoyed for the next few days. Or someone will suggest Angie not pay at all; the others will get it for her. This happens occasionally. Which, while very sweet of them, makes her feel even worse.

Her decaf tea arrives. Just to give her something to do with her hands.

The other couples are the Troutmans and the Dolans. Angie doesn't know the Dolans very well. They're friends of friends. There's a real possibility that Angie will never see them again. The restaurant itself—chosen this week by Wes—is low-ceilinged and darkly paneled. There are no windows visible from their round table in this corner of the room. Strings of white lights are tacked up along the molding, illuminating framed portraits of strangers from other eras. It's a table for eight. The chair to Angie's left is unoccupied.

The food was pretty good, Angie must admit, though she isn't sure she'd come back.

"I'm thinking about jamming some dough into Kevin's . . . bar, or whatever it is," Wes is saying now. His armpits strain against his sport coat. "Gotta be a tax write-off, if nothing else, right?"

So, okay, he's moved on from the stock market to taxes and their son's fancy new business venture, an establishment in Middletown that brews its own beer and serves small, overpriced plates prepared by some up-and-coming chef from the city. Gastropub, Angie thinks is the word for it. The Funderburkes scoff when they talk about it, as if it's all just some frivolous side hustle the son will outgrow before he moves on to his real career as a hedge fund manager. She hasn't been there yet, but Angie knows the place is doing well. It's been written up in *Connecticut Magazine*'s "New & Noteworthy" column and is getting a ton of word-of-mouth all over social media. Angie has no idea where the kid got the money to open the place. Well, okay, not true—of course she knows where he got the money: from his parents. Or his grandparents. Maybe both. Whenever Kevin Funderburke and his entrepreneurial adventures arise in conversation Angie feels a clenching inside, a kind of soul nausea. She hates that the Funderburkes have the means to set their son up with his own hip, fun, publicly successful business, and Angie doesn't; she hates that the Funderburkes have at least one kid who has stayed in Connecticut who they can see on weekends and holidays and for grandkids' birthday parties or even just dinner on a Wednesday; and, in her darkest, most shamefully hidden moments, she hates that Wes Funderburke, with his enormous belly and chronic hypertension and mysterious polyps, is still alive, while Jim, seemingly healthy as a horse for seventy years, is not.

She wouldn't mind a splash of milk in her tea, but it's all the way on the other side of the table, and she doesn't feel like asking for it.

"I need to get home."

It's Betty Troutman, leaning in from Angie's right, her voice barely above a whisper. Betty has a pretty, youthful face (if a bit over-Botoxed), but a severe man's haircut, dyed reddish brown. Tonight, she's wearing big, colorful earrings of a complicated geometric shape and a gray wool poncho. Whenever she uses her fork, she needs to flip the poncho out of the way to free her arm.

"Those mussels," she says, "are not sitting right. I . . . I need a bathroom."

"Oh no," Angie says, keeping her voice down. "Just go here."

Betty looks over her shoulder as if checking for spies. "I'd rather not. It could—"

"What are you two conspiring about over here?" Betty's husband Ron leans his elbows on the table, stretching around his wife to see Angie. "Plotting a coup, are we?"

Ron Troutman is a nice enough guy, if a bit stiff and formal—Jim used to say Ron would get visibly annoyed if you cleared your throat during a backswing or walked through his putting line—but Angie has never seen that side of him. To her, he just seems like a nervous guy who plans one joke or witty thing to say ahead of time and then picks an inappropriate point in the evening to awkwardly break it out.

"It's nothing, dear," Betty says, not turning toward her husband. "Don't worry about it."

Ron stays leaning on his elbows, holding his smile, unsure of what to do next. He's wearing a brand-new, button-down shirt, right out of the box, creases clearly visible. Angie feels a jolt of pity for the man. Finally, he leans back and shifts toward Wes Funderburke, who now appears to have switched the conversation to the perils of lawn chiggers.

Betty puts a hand to her mouth. A thin layer of sweat glistens on her forehead. "This is—oh my God, this is so embarrassing—this is an *emergency*, Ange."

"Come on." Angie feels around under Betty's poncho for her hand, then pushes her chair out and stands. "We'll be right back," she announces to the table.

Betty stands too, gingerly, gripping Angie's hand, trying to relax her face. She attempts a smile that comes off looking more like a sneer.

The other two women, Carol Funderburke and Judy Dolan, glance at each other. *Are we being left out of something?* they're probably wondering. The thought, Angie finds, is kind of exhilarating. She gives Betty's hand a tug and they head off toward the bar.

"I don't want to do this here," Betty is saying, real fear in her voice.

"Don't worry," Angie says. "I'll stand guard outside the bathroom door. No one's getting past. You'll have complete privacy."

"Oh good Lord."

They circle around the bar to the back hallway, Betty squeezing Angie's hand harder as they go. There is only one single-use bathroom. Angie tries the doorknob; it's locked. Betty groans.

"Don't worry," says Angie, and begins banging on the door with the heel of her fist. "Excuse me. *Excuse me!* We have an emergency out here!"

"I'm going to die," Betty says. "I'm going to kill myself."

"Oh, stop that." Angie keeps banging on the door. "For goodness' sake, Betty."

Lately, Angie has found herself snapping into abrupt, silent annoyance with people for routine indiscretions—a mix-up at the pharmacy, her granddaughter sleeping till noon, her mailman's occasional late arrival, Wes Funderburke—and she recognizes it happening now: the mussels aren't agreeing with Betty. She's embarrassed. It's not a big deal. At least Angie's aware of this about herself. That's got to count for something, right?

"It'll be fine, honey," she says now, gently. "Just hang on."

Finally, the bathroom door opens, and a big-chested, middle-aged woman fills the space. The woman's hair is pulled back so tightly her eyebrows seem to be lifted upwards from the tension. "Rude," the woman mutters.

"Yeah, sorry. But seriously—" Angie makes a shooing motion with her hand. "Out of the way. We have a situation here."

The woman steps slightly, grudgingly, to one side, opening up a narrow strip of space in the doorway. She's wearing a flimsy, loose-fitting, shiny top, and her breasts are so big that the top's fabric drops straight down from them as if plummeting off a cliff, giving the woman's torso a boxy, rectangular shape. She looks like a LEGO-person.

"Seriously?" Angie says. "We're gonna do *this* now? Listen, this woman is in *distress*. Will you please move?"

The woman waits a beat, then another. Her eyebrows try to squeeze into a scowl, then, reluctantly, she steps fully aside. "Rude," she says again before shuffling off.

Angie pushes the door all the way open and flicks on the light. The walls are painted a soft periwinkle, which is nice, but there's another one of those black-and-white, old-timey portraits of a stranger on one of the walls, which is weird. She turns to Betty. "Okay, there we are. Totally private. Now off you go."

"Don't listen."

Angie puts her fingers in her ears. "I'm just on guard duty."

Betty takes a deep breath and holds it—the expression on her face looks like someone being pinched—then slides past Angie and closes the door. The lock clicks, the faucet begins to run.

Murmured voices float down the hallway from the bar. A Beatles song—the one that repeats *"life goes ooooon"*—plays softly on the speaker system. For a moment, Angie feels good, then catches herself feeling good and recognizes the meaninglessness of that joy. Still, it's nice what she's doing now, helping Betty out this way. Once, a couple of years ago, when Jim was still here, Angie was playing in one of her bridge leagues at someone's house—she can't remember whose—and sometime toward the end of the evening, after several bottles of chardonnay had been opened and emptied, one of the women posed the question, "If you could go back in time, back to when you were twenty or twenty five years old, and remarry your husband, would you do it?"

There were about a dozen women there set up around multiple tables in the dining room (it was the Funderburkes' house, now that Angie thinks about it, that giant dining room of theirs), with teams rotating from table to table to play different opponents throughout the evening. And only three women—Angie, Betty, and one other woman, Laurie Wells, who has since moved to Norwalk—said that, yes, of *course* they'd marry their husbands if given the chance to go back and do it again. It was a silly, wine-fueled discussion really, but Angie remembers the enthusiasm with which all the other women (including Carol Funderburke) expounded upon their reasoning for why they would *never* marry their husbands again if offered a do-over. The conversation grew animated, everyone talking over each other, trying to one-up the previous illustration of spousal inadequacy. Hilarity ensued.

Angie kept quiet, wondering, *Could this be for real? Maybe they're joking.*

But no, this was how they really felt.

All of those husbands are still alive, walking around in the world, continuing to be inadequate disappointments. Except for Jim.

When it's you, then you'll know, Angie thinks. *Then you'll know what it's like.*

But, then again, maybe not. Maybe they *won't* know. Maybe they'll never know. Maybe the dull, aching emptiness living inside Angie day after day will, for them, be *relief*.

Behind the bathroom door, the toilet flushes loudly. The tenor of the running faucet changes when Betty washes her hands, then turns off. Angie prepares her face, hoping to appear welcoming and sympathetic, yet also to convey a sense of normalcy, of putting this behind them and getting back to life. The bathroom door opens. Betty switches off the light and stands in the doorway, looking exhausted and haggard. Her poncho hangs crookedly to one side. The ring of hair framing her face is damp from sweat or maybe from having splashed water on her face, or both.

"That was," Betty says, her voice raspy, "brutal."

Angie laughs. She can't help it. Just an unintentional bark at first, but then she has to cover her mouth, unable to hold it back.

"I mean, really just . . . *catastrophic*," Betty says, and then she's laughing too, and they reach out and take each other's hands to steady themselves and keep laughing, the occasional snort slipping out until the laughter finally subsides and they can catch their breath. And then they're standing there, holding hands in the hallway, eyes moist with tears.

Finally, Betty dabs at the corner of her eye with a knuckle and says, "I'm thinking those were the last mussels I'll ever eat in my life."

"Probably wise."

"We must never speak of this."

"Speak of what?"

Betty smiles. A man enters the hallway and makes his way toward them. The man is in his forties, movie-star handsome, fit and trim, full head of swept-back, grey-flecked hair, sleeves rolled up to mid forearm, an expensive-looking but unpretentious watch on his wrist. They watch him approach for a moment, then Betty takes Angie by the arm. "Yikes," she says. "Let's get out of here before he goes in."

They sidestep the man, who nods cordially to them, and head back through the bar, still holding onto each other, moving quickly as if fleeing a crime scene. Back at the table, the waiter is tallying up the bill. As Angie and Betty approach their chairs, everyone looks up at them, oddly expectant.

"Well, there they are!" Wes exclaims. "So, what kind of hijinks have you ladies been up to?" He laughs impishly, "Heh heh heh."

Betty's face twitches. "Oh," she stammers, "we, uh . . ."

Angie reaches out and snatches the check from the waiter's hand. "This is on me," she says, then starts digging around for her credit card in her purse, which hangs off the back of her chair. There's a moment of stunned silence, and then everybody starts talking at once.

"Angie, no—"

"Out of the question!"

"We couldn't let you—"

"That's really not neces—"

Angie waves them off. "I insist," she says, finally locating her credit card. "Please, let me do this." She hands the check and her card to the waiter and gives him a nod that she hopes says, *I'm in charge here. You can listen to me.* He takes the card and heads off with it.

"Angie," Wes says. "Really—"

"Nope, it's done. I want to." She sits, feeling charged and buoyant. "You all—I can't tell you how much it means that you continue to include me. I just want to say thanks. I've *been* wanting to. Please, let me do this for you all."

Betty settles in her chair and squeezes Angie's knee under the table. "Thanks, Ange."

"Yes, thank you, Angie," says Wes, and raises his glass of Sambuca. "Cheers."

No one again asks where she and Betty have been. When the receipt is placed down in front of her to sign, Angie tips thirty percent.

***

The drive from the restaurant in West Hartford to her house in Marlborough should take her about twenty minutes. Earlier in the day, the Troutmans offered to pick her up, but Angie declined, and now she's glad she did. Sitting in the back seat of the Troutmans' car would have felt awkward, plus now she has the luxury of sitting alone in the sweet hum of her own car—she still drives a minivan, just for herself—cruising through the darkness. She merges onto Route 2, radio off, the dashboard's glow on her face, and feels a feathery warmth move through her. Maybe she should call one of her kids to pass the time? Her daughter is in Charlotte with her lawyer husband and two children. Might be someone's bedtime, though; she probably shouldn't get in the middle of that. Her oldest son is in Tampa, but talking to him always fuels Angie's anxiety. He's "working from home" as a PR rep, though Angie suspects he's actually "between jobs" as a PR rep. She also suspects he and his wife aren't getting along, fighting over the causes of their son's recent delinquent behavior, shuttling the boy from therapist to therapist. Phone conversations with him can be taxing, in other words, and Angie doesn't want to sabotage her mood. Her youngest son is single and works for Spotify in Amsterdam. He might have some fun things to share with her—tales of his latest European travels or Danish women he's recently dated—but it's three in the morning over there. So that's out too.

She doesn't think she has any plans for tomorrow. She'll have to check her calendar.

Maybe she should clean out the closet in the back bedroom.

She could take the dog for a long walk if the weather's okay.

She exits Route 2, and as she turns onto Route 66, a two-lane country road cutting through fifty miles of central Connecticut, her headlights sweep across a stand of thin trees and underbrush and illuminate a bright set of glittering, ghostly eyes. The eyes belong to an animal of some sort—though she's never seen an animal like this before—standing on four legs in the gravel just off the road, low to the ground, looking back over its shoulder at her. The head is weasel-like, the body long and curved and dark, the legs short but somehow longer than they need to be. Angie's blood shivers. Oh God, she's seeing things. That is not a real animal. It's . . . mythological. Or extinct. Or *should* be extinct. It holds there in the beam of her headlights, momentarily arrested, and the headlights glide past it as she completes the turn back to the road ahead, and then it's as if the animal never existed; only the image of it remains, burned into her brain.

Angie realizes she's been holding her breath and struggles for a moment to take in air. She considers pulling over, regrouping, but she wants to put some distance between herself and the animal. She's only a couple minutes from home. She touches her own cheek and forehead, feeling a startling absence. *This* is what she misses most, what she longs for: being able to turn to someone—to Jim—and say, *Did you see that thing? What in the world was that?* She understands now that it's possible for fear to be thrilling when shared. Yes, that's what she misses.

She makes the final turn onto her street, and wonders if she'll ever get used to the permanence of Jim being gone, the terrible truth of it. She supposes not, yet for the first time she feels a strange, hopeful comfort in this knowledge.

Maybe she'll tell Betty about the animal tomorrow. Or one of her kids. It won't be the same, though. She knows this. There will be a loneliness in the telling. Maybe this time, she thinks, she'll just keep the memory for herself.

Milk Teeth

by Mackenzie Hurlbert

After losing her daughter in the grey days of April, Edith Thompson took to gardening. For those first few weeks, after the wake and funeral where a half-sized casket cradled her child, after the heavy-scented flowers disintegrated into piles of crunchy petals and rigid stalks, Edith reached into the earth. While her husband Ned sat at the kitchen table eating a casserole from a well-meaning neighbor, Edith wandered to her backyard and sifted through the dirt.

She bought seeds—tomato, watermelon, pepper, poppy— that rattled in their paper packets. Edith placed each one gently in finger-deep divots, and in June, after no green tips emerged from the soil, she purchased a tray of zucchini and cucumber sprouts, and planted them one by one along the garden's edge.

"Edith, honey, they're too close," Ned said when he found her one morning kneeling in the dark soil. She sat back on her heels. A wandering hand passed her cheek, leaving a streak of dirt.

"They'll cross-pollinate. You'll have a bunch of mutant squash-cucumbers trying to take over the world!" Ned bugged out his eyes like he once did for their daughter Allie when he was telling a scary story.

Edith shrugged. Once placed, she patted soil around their bases, tucking them in with a concentrated effort.

145

Within two weeks, the sprouts' leaves turned a toxic yellow. Each night after dinner, Edith watched their wasted forms from the window over the sink while Ned packed up the leftovers.

He tried to help. When Edith left to go to what she would only refer to as "the doctor's," he'd run the hose and soak the soil, hoping for some hint of green. These doctor visits were getting more and more frequent, and though Edith didn't say much, Ned hoped they were appointments with the therapist in town. Edith had stopped eating, rejected his affections, and refused to say Allie's name. The vibrant, playful woman he married lived limp and deflated—a glove without a hand.

It was during one of Edith's appointments when Ned found the teeth. They'd been stored in the top drawer of the kitchen island, wrapped in a thin sandwich bag cinched shut with one of Allie's butterfly-baubled hair ties. He undid the tie and poured the three milk teeth into his palm. Their jagged bottoms had once been tucked beneath his daughter's gums, sharp as a broken bottle. He couldn't believe how light they were. And fragile. He thought of her small, white hand in his. Alone in the kitchen, Ned let out a breath and felt his throat tighten.

Closing his eyes, Ned clasped the teeth in his fist. He couldn't remember the sound of his daughter's voice. The truth of it pierced him. He slammed his fist on the counter and felt the teeth bite into the flesh of his palm. Collapsing on the kitchen floor, he leaned up against the bottom cabinets and cried into the crook of his arm. He rode out the flow of grief as he always did—expelling it all in these moments of privacy.

When it had passed, Ned wiped the tears from his cheeks with his knuckles and focused on his breathing. His fist ached, and when he unfurled his fingers, he could see the teeth had broken the skin. They were tinged pink with blood. He whispered Allie's name to them. He felt the air electrify. He remembered her giggling in the grass outside—in fact, he could almost hear it. His breath caught. Then the neighbor started his lawn mower.

Tucking the hair tie and plastic baggie with its contents into his breast pocket, Ned headed outside to water Edith's dying zucchini plants. Returning the teeth meant risking the chance Edith would uncover them. They could trigger a breakdown, Ned thought, and he'd find her crying in the shower again, or she'd withdraw even more, sinking into herself. He could flush them down the toilet, but no . . . they were a part of Allie. He heard Edith's car creak into the driveway and groan to a halt.

Kneeling down, Ned pulled the baggie from his pocket and tightened the tie. Using one hand, he dug a hole as deep as he could in the loose soil and placed the teeth far into the shadows. Plowing the dirt back into place, he brushed off his hands and rose to his feet. Edith was behind him. He felt her heaviness.

"Hey, hon," he said, turning around. "How was the doctor's?"

Edith blinked off his greeting. Her small frame was lost in the folds of her dress. A paper bag hung from a limp hand at her side.

"What are you doing?" she asked, taking in his dirty knees and the nearby hose.

Ned cleared his throat. "Just figured I'd water the plants for you . . . and then, you know, I thought I saw something popping up. Like a sprout from those seeds you planted."

Edith barked a laugh without smiling. Ned didn't know that was possible. She turned to the house, and he took a few big steps to reach her side. "How was work?" he asked.

"It was work. You? There was a shipment today, right?" She kept her eyes on the ground.

"It was ok. Roger called in sick, so I had to cover his load and mine, but I got out early 'cause the new kid helped. They think next week . . ." He drifted off. She wasn't listening. Edith took quicker steps, and he let her get away. At the doorway, he kicked the dirt off of his shoes and brushed the soil from his knee. He followed her inside.

"Edith?" he said.

"Ned?" She put her bag on the counter and turned to face him.

"I miss her too, you know. But she loved you. She wouldn't want to see you like . . . All Allie wanted to do was make you smile—"

"Just stop," Edith said. Showing her back to him, she went about putting away the groceries.

That night Ned woke to an empty bed. Edith was outside, kneeling in the dirt and hunched over something. Her back heaved, and Ned guessed she was sobbing. He thought about going down there, placing his hand on her bare shoulder, and guiding her back to bed. Instead, he slipped back under the comforter. When he woke up, Edith had already left for work, and the only trace that she returned after her visit to the garden was the sheets on her side, smudged with soil.

***

A few days passed before Ned went back to water the garden, and there it was. Just a sprout, a tiny green spike emerging from the earth. It was just a little thing, but it looked healthy—vigorous even—when compared with the shriveled zucchini remains. When Edith got home that night, he brought it up: "Edith, did you see the garden today?"

His wife shrugged. "No. Why?"

"There's a sprout."

She looked at the space over his head. "Oh please."

"Edith! There's a sprout. You've grown something!"

She didn't believe him and ventured outside in her bare feet to see for herself. The green seemed to glow in the beam of her flashlight.

Ned hugged her. "I don't know what took, but we've got a green little sprout. Isn't that great? I knew there was something wrong with those cucumber plants."

Edith stared at the tilled earth for a moment before smiling a soft, sad smile of relief. "Yeah, it's good news, Ned. It's good."

***

The sprout grew visibly each day. Within two weeks, it had spread across the tilled earth of their garden in a tangle of thorny stems and vines. Every night, Edith went out to tend to it, gliding under the moonlight in her white shift. Ned pretended not to notice, changed the sheets when they got dirty, and mopped up her footprints in the morning. Edith started to smile more. Her face regained color—a glow even—and her figure started to soften. There were fewer and fewer doctor's visits, and one night they even made love before going to sleep, something they hadn't done in months.

By mid-July, the plant filled the entire plot, and its leaves multiplied, thickening into an impenetrable mass. Ned clipped away at the tendrils that reached beyond the garden's edge, but other than that, Edith cared for it—watering it daily and showering it with green pellets of fertilizer-like confetti. The plant's all-consuming presence weighed on Ned—he couldn't shake it from his thoughts. Its ever-shifting shape seemed to observe them from the backyard like a stranger behind the curtains. He noticed there were no flowers or buds—just leaves with serrated edges that clung to their clothes like Velcro—and thorny, thick vines that leaked milky sap when pruned. Ned's stomach turned with the thought of it. He found the plant had a smell—a heavy, humid stench like overripe bananas. But Edith didn't seem to mind. When Ned mentioned it, she laughed and told him he was sniffing too many exhaust fumes from the delivery truck.

Edith would visit the plant after dark and walk circles around it as Ned watched from their bedroom window. She'd return to bed with its putrid scent in her hair. When Ned kissed her goodbye in the morning, he could swear he tasted it on her lips.

By August, the plant had grown a head taller than him and cast a shadow over their yard. Ned was finding its leaves everywhere—in the shower, under the couch, and clinging to the back of his uniform for work. Edith wore its scent as a perfume, but she smiled more. She kissed him good morning with a new intensity and had rediscovered her old laugh, the one that had made him fall in love with her. While her happiness was a relief to him, Ned knew he was not the cause of this change and couldn't help but eye the plant with envy.

During one of Edith's late-night walks, Ned awoke to a giggle. He heard it—a long, lilting giggle. He sat up, alone in bed, and listened. After a few beats of silence, he walked over to the window to look out on the yard. Edith had dropped to her knees beside the plant and was reaching into it as if petting something or tickling it. Ned slipped on his shoes and went down to see what she was doing. When he was standing on the grass behind her, he could hear she was singing "You Are My Sunshine," a tune she used to hum to Allie. He couldn't see what her hands were touching. The leaves of the plant had engulfed Edith's arms past her elbows.

In a breathy soprano, she sang, "You make me happy, when skies are grey . . ." Ned swallowed hard. Hearing Edith sing those words again flooded his mind with memories of Allie's nursery—the creak of the rocker, the softened darkness that smelled of powder and baby.

"What are you doing?" he asked.

Edith yelped but laughed. "Damn it, Ned," she said. "You scared me!" She withdrew her arms from the plant and stood up, brushing the dirt from her knees. One of the plant's leaves stuck to the hem of her nightdress.

"Jesus, Edith, look at your arms." Her forearms were covered with scratches, thin red lines where thorns must have caught her. "What were you thinking?"

"I was just singing to it," Edith said, slipping her hand into his and guiding him back toward the house. She looked years younger under the moonlight. Luminescent. Magical. "I was telling my doctor about it, and he said plants grow stronger if you sing to them." She squeezed his hand.

Ned left his hand in hers but did not return the squeeze. "At two in the morning, though?"

Edith smiled and shrugged. "I couldn't sleep." With that she let go of his hand, pecked his cheek, and bounded into the house. When he found her upstairs, he pulled her into the bathroom and washed her scratched arms with cotton swabs and peroxide. She didn't flinch at the sting.

"What were you reaching for in there?" Ned said, returning the bottle of peroxide to the bathroom cabinet. His wife sat on the toilet and watched him, smiling.

"I thought I saw something," she said.

"Like what?"

"I'm not sure. It was dark." Edith let out a wide yawn, not bothering to cover her mouth. Her full lips, her flushed cheeks. Ned barely recognized this person. Even so, when he reached their bed and she greeted him with warm hands, he embraced her all the same. It was like making love to a complete stranger, and afterwards, Edith fell asleep naked in their tangle of sheets and Ned stared at the ceiling, feeling satisfied but guilty.

***

September brought what Ned expected to be the most challenging hurdle they'd faced since the funeral—Allie's birthday. It was this time the previous year when the doctors found the tumor, and Allie had spent her ninth, and last, birthday with that diagnosis looming over her. Diagnosis—such a big word for an eight-year-old. They brought her to the city zoo and botanical gardens, where they watched her ride an elephant and feed a giraffe. Ned could still hear her laughter as the giraffe's blue tongue curled around her small hand.

They walked through the tropical plants in the greenhouse, and she had Ned smell all the flowers. Edith and Allie posed for a photo by the koi pond, Allie's green eyes popping among the foliage and Edith's thin, forced smile obvious and transparent. They visited the gift shop before they left, and Ned told Allie to pick out a souvenir. While she was debating between a stuffed lemur and a hat with tiger ears, Edith started to cry again and had to go outside. He ended up buying Allie both and then threw in some cotton candy, which she devoured on the ride home.

With the distraction of the plant outside, Edith and Ned didn't discuss the approaching date. Ned avoided the topic, partially out of the fear that any mention of Ally would send Edith spiraling. But more so, he couldn't fight the tendril of spite worming its way through the back of his mind. Part of him hoped Edith would forget—too busy mothering the plant to remember the anniversary. He could wait and not mention it. He could grieve privately as he had done all along—which, if he was honest, was how he preferred it. Especially now. Especially now that, for Edith, mothering a plant had apparently replaced what she'd decided was the unbearable memory of mothering their real child. So he stayed silent and threw himself into his work, covering late shifts as much as he could. Edith tended to the garden.

The plant's height had more than doubled in the past few

weeks, and in order to support it, the stems had thickened into trunks. On the night before Allie's birthday, Ned pretended to sleep as his wife slipped out of bed once more. He sat up and watched through their bedroom window as Edith walked across the lawn and knelt beside the plant. Its shadow had grown so deep that, when Edith left the moonlit yard to stand and then kneel at the garden's edge, Ned could only just make out her pale shape. He could see her gesturing, as if she was having a conversation. He watched as she leaned back and laughed. Sour jealousy bloomed in his chest. He didn't even bother to put his shoes on—and was down the stairs and on the grass beside her in moments. The moon had slipped behind a cloud, and all was dark.

"Edith, honey, this is enough." He kept his voice flat, a tone he never used with her. She stayed facing the plant as if he'd said nothing.

"You're worrying me," he said, a bit softer this time, and stepped forward to rest a hand on her bare shoulder. She shuddered at his touch.

"What time is it?" she asked.

"Past one," Ned told her. "Let's go to bed."

Edith shook her head. "She was born at 1:11. I remember. 1-1-1, an angel number. A lucky number." She looked up at Ned, and in her grey eyes he saw pain, and anger, and defiance. But most of all, a bottomless sadness. He knelt down beside her in the grass and wrapped his arms around her cold shoulders.

"I miss her too," he said.

With those words, the moon emerged again, and the plant began to shift as if fidgety with nerves. Leaves rustled, vines bent, and soon the entire garden seemed to shudder with energy. They stood, and Ned took a step back as the vines of the plant reached out, extending up into the air and to either side. Leaves shook free and fell around them, Velcroing to their clothes and hair. The stems of the plant bent to the left and right. Ned could hear a deep groan, but he wasn't sure if it had come from the plant or Edith.

In front of them, the plant parted to form a path. The moonshine illuminated a clearing at the end, the heart of the garden. Edith stepped forward, and Ned reached to grab her hand. Something was moving at the end of the path; he could see it. He meant to pull Edith back, to guide her to the house, back to their bed where they could fall asleep and wake up in the morning and pretend it all had been a dream. But when he saw the movement in the moonlight—the pulse of a presence, of life—he took her hand. Barefoot, they passed between the walls of thorns and leaves.

As they entered the clearing, they saw what had moved. It was a giant bud hanging three feet off the ground and pulsing offbeat as if something inside was struggling to escape. Ned reached out, placing his palm against its soft outer skin. It was warm against his hand. He could feel something inside shifting beneath the thick layers of flesh. Edith touched it too, smiling as the bud pulsed again, swinging toward her. "It's her," she said, meeting Ned's gaze with wide eyes. She smiled and looked back to the bud.

Ned couldn't speak. He wanted Allie back—wanted to remember her voice and how her hand felt in his. His gaze fell to Edith's arms, lined with scratches, and he inhaled the sour, putrid scent of rotten fruit. How could something he wanted so much smell so wrong?

"Come on home, honey," Edith said. The bud jerked hard, swaying a bit in the air. Ned pulled Edith back by the shoulder and stood at the edge of the clearing with his arms wrapped tightly around her. They watched as one fleshy outer layer unfurled and then another. The sour stench filled the air, but Ned was too overwhelmed to gag. Emerging from the wet, flexing petals of the bud was a child, slippery and bare in the moonlight. A soft white child's foot dropped to the grass, and then another. Legs thin like reeds. The small impression of a navel. With one large pulse, the bud birthed the child into the night, and it collapsed in a slick heap on the grass.

Ned and Edith were frozen as the child, shivering, rose to its knees. Its eyes were closed. Its hair, dark with the bud's slime, clung to its cheeks, neck, and shoulders. It looked innocent to Ned, just a small child's face with closed eyes and a pink mouth. It tilted to meet the moonlight and parted its lips, and then its eyes opened, and they were green just like Allie's. Ned choked back a sob. Edith clapped, laughing, and the child's face grinned, showing the pearly white caps of teeth.

Edith held out her hand, but the child didn't move. Instead, the walls of vines and leaves around them shuddered, and a thorny tendril broke free to reach toward Edith's waiting palm. It wrapped in a coil around her wrist. Ned watched as thorns bit flesh.

"Hi, Sunshine," Edith whispered, smiling as the tendril tightened and cut deeper. Blood fell in quick drops to the ground at her feet. A dark tongue escaped the child's mouth, wetting Allie's lips and leaving them glistening in the moonlight.

"Hi, Mama," it said in a familiar voice. In fact, it was so familiar and similar to Allie's, the voice he'd forgotten, that it made his heart flip—yet as those two words hung in the night air, Ned knew that this was not his daughter. Though soft and sweet, the words carried a cavernous echo—a hollow, inhuman sound that hid behind Allie's voice like rot beneath a floorboard.

He watched Allie's gaze shift to him and squeezed his eyes shut. Ned felt a leaf tickle the bare skin at the base of his neck. He heard that same hollow voice say, "Hi, Papa."

Ned hadn't screamed since he was a child, but when he did, it was a tiger's roar that shook the trees. He sank into the black depths behind his eyelids. He heard the lilting giggle of a girl in the grass and his wife's soft soprano. ♦

Wicked Blues

by Crystal D. Mayo

There is no life here. No scent of jasmine nor the smell of God's breath right after a rainstorm. No flashes of light capturing moments nor laughter that crescendos out into hallways. There is only a stranger lying between starched white sheets. Her eyes searching upward toward Savannah light she will never see again.

I have stood over her bed a million times. I know her face. Each feature a snapshot in my mind. The way her lips part when she finally surrenders to deep slumber. The way her eyelids slightly rustle like soft wind as the first rays of dawn yawn across her face. She was my mother and every nuance of her face belonged to me. Grandma Ojo always joked that my daddy spit my older sister, Yara, right out of him. When I was little I thought that saying was nasty 'cause can't no beauty brew inside the phlegm of a grown man's spit. But as my sister got older, what my grandma said was true. Grandma Ojo told us stories of the younger version of Daddy courting Momma, how when Momma opened the door, Daddy stood with lanky legs in the frame, looking like a tall glass of water. His ripples made Momma's friends swoon, but his name was written all over her. Yara inherited his etched cheekbones, silky dark hair, and legs dipped in molasses. When she walked into a room with her brazen curves, the boys who used to chase us round corners till their armpits left an odor of sour onions swooned. Grandma Ojo warned Yara not to fool around with those ripe-for-the-pickin' boys but her name was written all over them.

I wasn't tall or a rippling glass of water, my face belonged to Momma. I prayed I would grow up into her rare eclectic beauty. In family photographs she never sat in the center 'cause she always sat quietly in the background until your eyes noticed hers. And when they did she was breathtaking. Her pecan tan skin was the canvas for her freckles, which scattered across her face just right.

Folks say the life of the house is in the kitchen, but in ours it was in Momma's bedroom. On cool summer days I'd sit on the floor by the edge of her bed with crossed legs and the shea butter jar between my thighs. While she greased my roots I pulled out old family photo albums. I appointed myself the griot in the family, listening as I turned the pages and Momma shared each detail of the branches that made up our family tree. Daddy got his height from Great-Granddaddy Cyrus, a solider who fought in World War II. Great-Grandma Lucinda, Grandma Ojo's momma, was a midwife and herbal doctor. Back then Black folks couldn't get their foot into medical school so she healed her own people in the comfort of their homes. Expectant mothers drank boiled green Spanish moss tea for an easier childbirth. Elders suffering from swellings and joint pain got relief from a rubbing of cayenne pepper and aloe juice.

Daddy knew the first time he had fallen in love with Momma was when the sunlight danced across her face under a cherry tree. When they married he built our house from the ground, brick by brick, so that he knew it would have a solid foundation. Although they shared the bedroom, he built it just for her, he painted the ceiling blue and added a skylight so that each time she woke he could see morning light dance across her face. Every day the sun shone it would remind him of why he had fallen in love with her in the first place. He never told me that, but since I was the family griot, that is the way I'm gonna tell it.

Before she got sick, Momma's room was filled with shelves of homemade potions that Yara and me dabbed on our necks and collarbones. The sweet scents lingered until the next morning.

The walls were filled with black-and-white moments in time in silver and gold frames. Most of them were of me and Yara, Momma's favorite works of art. My favorite was of all of us lying in her bed. Momma in the middle with Daddy on one side of her and Yara on the other. I was five, resting on top of Momma's chest, looking straight into the camera, the sunlight illuminating all of our faces. Momma never gave a title to that picture or any others she took, for that matter. She said that black-and-white photos made your eyes see beyond the picture, and once they did, you would have to name what you saw for yourself. Daddy named our picture *The Mother Tree*. Mother trees are the glue that hold all the trees in a forest together. Me, Yara, and Daddy were Momma's leaves.

The walls of Momma's room were sacred, they held artifacts between their cement and mortar. Every crack and crevice held our laughter, which crescendoed through the house.

When it was just me and Momma, I'd sprawl across her lilac-scented bedsheets and rest my head against the bend of her arm. Together we listened to the rhythm of summer rain playing against the skylight. When the storm was over, we'd open every window and lie back in the bed with our eyes closed, breathing the outside air deep into our lungs. If someone had taken a picture of us in that moment, the title would have been *The Smell of God's Breath after a Rainstorm*.

Momma always said the best moments in our lives are never captured by a lens of a camera but in the memories of our minds. Like when we stared at ourselves in a handheld mirror, admiring the arch of our eyebrows, the slight imperfection of our left eyes, just a pinch smaller than the other. We ran our fingers across the arches of our noses down to the fullness of our lips that overstepped into our smile. I was her and she was me. But there was something in Momma's eyes. I'd get lost in swirls of cotton candy. But if I propped myself across her chest and looked straight into them long and hard enough, I saw the depths of her soul, deep, flowing like the Egyptian river. Sometimes, when her pupils turned the slightest shade of indigo, hidden in the edges of her eyelids I found the watery footprints of secrets she buried inside. I never asked what they were; I just blinked them into my eyes and kept them there.

But this banshee of a woman lying in front of me has barren eyes. No river of life runs through them. This woman is my double-walker, only a shadow of myself.

"Nora Rose," she calls me by my name but it doesn't pulsate the life, the memories I shared with *my momma*. The stranger in the bed reaches to wrap me in her arms. I flinch and step away.

Grandma Ojo yells at me. "In all my years of livin' I ain't never seen no daughter be so indifferent to her own momma!" It doesn't matter how many times Grandma Ojo banishes me to the rose garden to fetch a switch for the back of my thighs, it won't change the fact that she ain't my momma. Not even Daddy, who for twenty-five years had his name written all over her, believes me.

Tonight, as Yara sleeps peacefully at the foot of her bed, I'll lie awake with lit sage, guarding her from what lurks in the darkness.

She ain't my momma.

She is murk and gloom

and benighted black dust born—

from wicked blues. 🛡

Pain Management

by Chris Belden

It's the familiar voice that first alerts Carl that Dr. Allen has arrived at the funeral home. A garish, midwestern honk—as if a tiny amplifier were lodged in the man's sinus cavity. Carl hears it from around the corner where the line disappears and, according to several sources, snakes out the door into the parking lot. His father may have been a popular man in town, but Carl did not expect the family dentist to put in an appearance.

"Is that Dr. Allen?" he whispers to his mother, who stands next to him to receive the mourners. She's dressed in black, complete with a veil that covers her tear-puffed face. At the moment, having taken a Valium, she has it under control, though she moves slowly and occasionally slurs her words when responding to the endless condolences.

"He did your father's root canal not long ago," she tells him. Then she goes back to thanking people Carl only half recognizes.

The viewing room is the largest available at Schreiber & Sons. The walls are red, the carpet is red, the curtains are red. Carl feels like he's standing inside a huge mouth. In between shaking hands with old pals of his father's—former law partners and clients, neighbors from way back when—Carl keeps glancing at the doorway, waiting for Dr. Allen to appear. He hears the voice again, and though he can't quite make out the words above the buzz of the crowd in the viewing room, the tone is unmistakable. This is the voice that greeted Carl as a child every six months like clockwork with, "Okay, kiddo, open up, and let's take a peek at those teeth of yours!" The terror he would feel at that moment, and for the succeeding half hour or so, comes rushing back to him.

"I think I need a break," he tells his mother, and even through the veil he can detect her distress.

"Please don't," she whispers. "Don't leave me alone."

It's just the two of them here to receive the guests. Carl's older brother, Richie, remains missing, possibly dead himself from an overdose or some other unsafe behavior cooked up by his unwell mind. His father had been an only child, so there are no aunts or uncles to stand here in front of the coffin with them, no cousin to take a break with, to share a slug of booze with in the parking lot. Just Carl and his mother and all these people feeling sorry for them.

His father, sixty-seven, died suddenly of a rampant infection after knee-replacement surgery. A heavy drinker, and sedentary since his mandatory retirement two years ago, he was not able to fight off the infection that ate away at his compromised kidneys and liver, and then his lungs, leaving only his strong heart to hold the fort. It ticked away for a full week while the rest of him lay in a coma until, finally, it gave in. That was four days ago, and Carl still has not cried. He feels as numb as the man in the open coffin behind where he and his mother stand shaking hands and saying, over and over, "Thank you for coming."

Dr. Allen's voice grows louder as he nears the viewing room doorway. "I did *all* their teeth," Carl hears him saying, "for years and years." That voice—it cuts through the air like the hiss of a drill. Carl shivers, suddenly back in the dentist's dingy office: the sticky faux leather chair, the adjustable overhead lamp aimed directly into Carl's eyes, the tray lined with sharp, shiny metallic instruments. Even the smell returns to him, a combination of alcohol, mint mouthwash, and mold.

"So sorry for your loss," a man says as he clasps Carl's hand. It's Mr. Fletcher, one of his father's partners, but Carl only remembers him because he wears an eye patch—Richie used to call him Mr. Cyclops. Most of the faces here have started to blur together. Carl didn't even recognize Mrs. Caserta earlier, their neighbor for many years. She had aged so much, which for some reason surprised Carl. He wonders if maybe he hasn't lived long enough himself to accept such profound changes in people's appearances. He watched his own parents age gradually and never noticed the difference—until this past week. His mother was always active, lively, involved in charities—the Visiting Nurse Association, the Red Cross, the ASPCA—and yet here she stands, wobbly and white haired. An old lady. When did that happen? Would Dr. Allen look that old?

Of course, the dentist had already seemed ancient at the time—as did anyone his parents' age. He remembers the man's failed attempts at youthfulness—the wire-rimmed glasses that replaced his thick, black frames, the grown-out hair that replaced his military buzz cut, the striped trousers beneath his threadbare lab coat, the sad effort to grow a mustache. Carl also recalls the parade of pretty, mini-skirted young assistants who would stand to the side and hand Dr. Allen whatever he needed ("Hand me that curette, will ya, hon?"). None seemed to last from one six-month appointment to the next, but Carl always liked them, even before puberty pushed his eyes toward their cleavage as they leaned over him to hand Dr. Allen the chalky toothpaste. At the end of each appointment, the assistant would open a flat box filled with plastic rings, each in its own foam notch, from which Carl and Richie could choose. Richie favored the hologram rings that, when you moved your finger slightly, showed Tarzan or Superman lunging at some villain. Carl preferred the animal rings—dogs, cats, rabbits. He looked forward to these prizes, though they never truly made up for the torture he'd just endured at the hands of Dr. Allen.

He can't remember any overt sexual abuse. Just the occasional hand on his thigh, maybe an inch or so too close to his crotch, while the dentist asked how he'd been and if there were any teeth bothering him lately. Once, while examining a cavity toward the rear of Carl's wide-open mouth, he seemed to linger a strangely long time with his face just a couple of inches away. Carl wondered for a moment if the dentist was about to kiss him. These weird moments were not worth reporting to his mother, he decided, since by that point she would have achieved maximum exasperation due to Carl's pre-appointment whining. By the time the doctor's visit ended, she would be all too ready to hustle her boys out of there with zero tolerance for more complaints of any kind.

Unbelievable as it is to Carl now, Dr. Allen never used Novocain. Until he went to college, finally escaping his long-time dentist, Carl didn't know that a local anesthetic was even an option. Dr. Allen would simply announce to his assistant that the patient had a cavity, and she would break out the drill and filling material while the dentist asked Carl in a suggestive tone whether he had a girlfriend. "No," Carl always replied, nearly shivering in fear of the pain to come while Dr. Allen chuckled and squeezed his thigh, saying, "What? A good-looking lad like yourself? I don't believe it. Do _you_, Heather?" And the assistant would say, "Not at all. If he was a coupla years older, _I'd_ be his girlfriend," and Dr. Allen would laugh and tickle her while she set out the instruments of torture.

The hiss of the drill, the feeling of bone being ground away inside his head, the wandering hand—no wonder the dentist's voice gives Carl the willies even after all these years. And there he is, in the doorway now, looking remarkably the same, though perhaps shorter, a bit rounder, and only slightly less intimidating in a gray suit rather than the faded white lab coat. He's honking away to another guest about the Indians' chances at breaking even this season. "Not likely," he announces with a rueful laugh. "Not this year *or* next, I'm afraid."

Carl keeps one eye on Dr. Allen until he's just a few people away in line. By this point, he's finally clammed up, perhaps out of respect for the grieving family. Carl wishes Richie were here to stand with him. Yeah, maybe crazy Richie would know what to do, what to say. Maybe he'd confront Dr. Allen and publicly shame him for his behavior. *Is that what I should do?* Carl wonders. But he knows his mother would flip out if he made any kind of scene. And his father might just rise up out of his coffin, waxy and poorly made-up, to upbraid Carl for embarrassing his poor mother.

"My sincere condolences," Dr. Allen, now standing before him, says in a voice so soft that Carl barely recognizes it. The dentist extends a hand, and after a quick glance at his mother as if she might object to his grasping the same hand that once touched his thigh, Carl takes it, and the two men shake. Then Dr. Allen moves over to his mother, who thanks him for coming and for all the help over the years, including that root canal. She still has no clue, Carl thinks. She *never* had a clue.

"It was my pleasure," Dr. Allen says.

And then the next person in line arrives, takes Carl's hand, and says how deeply sorry she is.

After the line of mourners has finally exhausted itself, a number of people stick around to chat in the viewing room. Dr. Allen stands among them, his voice back to its foghorn level. Carl escorts his mother to a seat and excuses himself to use the restroom. On his way out, he glances at the coffin and remembers the moment a few weeks back when he visited his father in the hospital after his knee surgery. His father had managed to use the bathroom but was unable to pull up his pajama bottoms. "Do you mind helping?" he asked in a small, weary voice, and after some hesitation, Carl leaned down to pull the pajamas up over his father's bandaged knees and drooping genitals. He felt like he'd crossed a line into some new territory, and he still feels that way, lost and clueless.

In the men's room, Carl stands at one of the two urinals, relieved to be away from the crowd, from his mother, from his dead father. The room is blessedly empty—until the door creaks open and Dr. Allen parks himself at the next urinal.

Carl shuts his eyes and concentrates, but he cannot manage to pee. Dr. Allen, meanwhile, unzips, sets one hand on the wall, sighs, and lets loose a horse-like stream.

Carl stares straight ahead. He considers leaving but does not want to go through the pantomime of pretending he's successfully urinated—the wiggle, the zip up, the casual washing of hands. He's decided to wait this out, to let Dr. Allen finish up and go. But now he can sense his former dentist, midstream, looking at him. Carl turns his body slightly to the left, away from Dr. Allen, in case the old man tries to check out his junk.

"I feel like I owe you an apology," Dr. Allen says once he's stopped pissing.

"Uh . . ." Carl says. "Excuse me?"

"All those years," Dr. Allen says as he zips up, "I didn't use Novocain on you poor boys." He remains at the urinal next to Carl. "But I want you to know that it wasn't my idea."

Thoroughly confused now, Carl fully gives up. He zips his fly and turns to Dr. Allen, who suddenly seems small and insubstantial next to him, an old man in a wrinkled, cheap suit.

"It wasn't?" Carl asks.

"It was your father. He asked me not to use it."

"But why?"

Dr. Allen chooses this moment to move to the single sink, where Carl watches him wash his hands thoroughly—as if he's about to examine someone's mouth.

"He said he wanted to toughen you boys up," the dentist says. "That you needed to know pain."

"And my mom went along with that."

"Apparently. Though I definitely used it on *her*. Several times. *And* on your father."

Carl doesn't know what to say. He recalls how his father would get exasperated if he complained about the drillings until, finally, Carl stopped talking about it, which was probably the goal all along.

"I always felt bad for you boys," Dr. Allen says. "Maybe I should have ignored him, but then he'd see it on the invoice, and, well . . ." He shrugs.

Carl notices how Dr. Allen keeps referring to "you boys," and he wants to say, "What do you mean, '*you boys*?'" when it was always just *Carl* getting a filling, sometimes two, which he considered profoundly unfair. He was diligent about brushing his teeth, unlike Richie, who often skipped brushing and yet seemed to never have a cavity.

But then an old memory floats up. Once, when Carl told Richie about Dr. Allen's hand on his thigh and how strange that made him feel, his brother said the dentist had touched his penis, which was "even weirder."

"Did you tell Mom?" Carl recalls asking. But Richie just shrugged and said, "Nah. She probably wouldn't believe me."

Carl hasn't thought of this exchange in ages, and he wonders how he could have forgotten such a thing. But then Richie hated to be outdone and would sometimes make patently outrageous claims. If Carl said he'd done ten push-ups, Richie would insist he'd done a hundred. If Carl rode his bike around the block no-handed, Richie rode a mile. At a certain point, Carl simply stopped believing his brother. But now—standing here in the bathroom with this old man—he asks himself, what if he *was* telling the truth? Though Richie was years away from his mental deterioration at the time, perhaps Dr. Allen could somehow detect his as-yet untapped madness and knew the boy wouldn't care all that much. Or maybe he just favored the happy-go-lucky brother with the good dental genes over shy, awkward Carl.

Dr. Allen puts his hand, still wet from the sink, on Carl's shoulder. "No hard feelings?"

The door opens and Mr. Fletcher enters the small restroom.

"Get your hands off me," Carl hisses at Dr. Allen.

"Excuse me?"

"You heard what I said." Carl turns to Mr. Fletcher. "This guy just tried to grope me."

The lawyer swivels his one eye from Carl to Dr. Allen.

"*What?*" the dentist says. "I did no such thing!"

"Get out of here, you pervert," Carl says, "before I call the police."

Dr. Allen steps back as if struck. Mr. Fletcher says to him, "I think you'd better go."

Staring at Carl, Dr. Allen opens the door. "I . . . I understand," he whispers. "You're grieving." And he exits.

"Are you okay, son?" Mr. Fletcher asks.

"Yes. I'm fine." After washing his hands for a very long time, Carl returns to his mother. Most of the guests have gone, including Dr. Allen, he notices. He sits down and finds he's shaking.

His mother is looking off toward the casket. Carl, too, stares at his father's profile, at the frown that the mortician was unable to rearrange. This is the last time, Carl realizes, that he will see what remains. The idea of his father's body lying six feet beneath the surface of the earth—in the pitch black—his thinning hair continuing to grow and his teeth—the teeth that Dr. Allen drilled with the aid of an anesthetic—remaining intact for decades . . . it knocks something loose inside Carl. He feels as lonely as he's ever felt.

He reaches over and takes his mother's hand. She squeezes, gives a tired smile, and says, "I wish your brother was here."

"Me too," Carl says. "Me too." 🛡

Morning Session

by Ken Cormier

He was sitting at his desk daydreaming. In his mind, he could see himself sitting at a desk and writing. It wasn't his desk. Maybe it was a desk from his past. Maybe a desk from his first marriage. There was a dog bed on the floor next to the desk—no dog. The floor was Hardwood, made of the wide planks you see in colonial homes, and there was a stone fireplace with glowing embers. He imagined a cup of tea, and then suddenly there it was, next to his hand. He wrote with a ball point pen on a legal pad. He seemed to be taking dictation. There was an urgent voice in the writing. It spoke in short, clipped sentences. There was no dialogue.

The narrator of the piece he was writing in the daydream was named Simon. Simon was an aspiring fiction writer who had drawn inspiration from, and written in great detail about, his older sister's descent into drug addiction and despair. While he was always pleased with the drama and the emotional arc of the scenes he had composed, he feared that if his sister were ever to read them, she would feel mortified and betrayed, and it would probably be too much for her fragile psyche to bear. Though he had rendered these scenes as fiction, changing all the characters' names, and fabricating settings and situations to disguise the true story, he knew that anyone even remotely familiar with him and his family would recognize the autobiographical elements in an instant.

Simon's sister was named Sarah, and he had idolized her as a child. In her first semester of college, Sarah had nearly died from an overdose of prescription pills. Simon was only ten when it happened. His parents had tried to shield him from all the mess, but he remembered seeing exactly what was happening. Even then, he felt like he understood the gravity of the situation. He disapproved of Sarah's actions, but only in the way he might disapprove of his own foibles and flaws—his sloppy room, for instance, or his tendency to daydream at school. Sometimes, though, as he grew older, he identified so closely with his older sister that he felt her tribulations were somehow his, and that he was living through her experiences—some of them, at least—just as intensely as she was. He romanticized her despair, wept quietly in his room, imagined the ways in which his own life's trajectory was bound for chaos and ruin. It was only a matter of time, he felt, before his sadness ruined him as it had ruined her. He wondered what his rock bottom would look like. Would he wander the streets, homeless and hungry and seeking out another high? Would he be institutionalized? Imprisoned? Perhaps Sarah, seeing what a mess he was making of his life, would finally overcome her own demons and focus her energies on helping him to recover. Could she somehow become his savior, in the same way that he always wished he could be hers? It was a feeling he would not be able to shake until, finally, in his mid-twenties, he would cut himself off entirely from his sister. After more than a decade of drug addiction, alcohol abuse, rehabilitation programs, incarcerations, promises, assurances, lies, and manipulations, it was finally time to separate himself from her negativity and self-destruction. She was his sister, he told himself, not his child.

And now it had been nearly ten years since he had spoken with her, yet whenever he sat down to write, she was all he could think about. He would inevitably draw from his memories of her as he constructed his sentences—the slow and steady cadences of her speaking voice, the shapeless thrift-store outfits she always wore, the way she could never finish telling a joke before collapsing into hysterical laughter, the sucking sound that her chest made when she cried. He did not want to write memoir, to expose his dirty little secrets for public consumption, but everything he wrote felt too close to the real thing. He called her Margaret, then Hilda, then Penelope, but it was always Sarah who shined through. He dressed her in overalls and gave her a club foot. Instead of a pill addict, he made her a glue sniffer. He turned himself into an older sister, or, in one draft, a sympathetic aunt. He killed off her father—*their* father—in a train accident, commuting to the city only months after she was born. This provided the seed for her troubles. It gave her something to ruminate on whenever she sat in a clinician's office, a group session, or a jail cell. But no matter how he tried to cloak it, it was always apparent that he was simply rendering his sister on the page.

For a time, Simon tried to write about different characters and subjects altogether. He made some progress on a story about a woman who for years had been the caretaker for a rental property on coastal Maine. The story moved slowly. She had a husband with a heart condition. Her old high school friend contacted her out of the blue one summer. The owner of the general store near the beach had been the best friend of a boy whom she'd once loved, and who had died tragically in a car accident in his early twenties. But about fifty pages into the narrative, it struck Simon that the sadness of this woman was, again, the sadness of Sarah. She was neither drug-addicted nor suicidal, but, like Sarah, she kept directing herself into dead ends, failing to meet up with her old friend as she had promised, averting her eyes from the store manager's friendly glances, and even quitting her position as caretaker under the false pretense that she had contracted a rare skin disease. This same thing happened when he tried to write a dystopian science fiction piece about humanoids with big, soft lavender ears whose world was gradually being transformed into a massive penal colony through a process of mind control and bodily fluid extraction. It didn't take long for Sarah to rear her head in the form of a recalcitrant prisoner who lashed out at her family when they visited her on state holidays, and soon she began to dominate the narrative in a way that began to actually frighten Simon. She transitioned from a minor character to the story's narrator/protagonist, appealing directly to the sympathies of the reader, propping herself up as an exemplar of authenticity and integrity even as she manipulated and betrayed those who loved and supported her most. She was willing, it seemed, to sacrifice everyone in pursuit of her selfish ends. It was as if Sarah were trying to communicate with Simon through his writing.

He switched gears again, this time creating a protagonist who wanted to write fiction but couldn't help writing directly about his own experience, especially about an older brother, who had been consumed with substance abuse problems and depression for as long as he could remember. All of this new protagonist's fiction ended up centering on characters that resembled his older brother, and he never felt comfortable sharing what he had written with anyone inside or outside his family. It was a predicament that, for a while, he felt he might be able to overcome, but as the months and years ticked by, he became increasingly convinced that he was helpless in the face of it. The protagonist's problem was exacerbated by the fact that he was an assistant professor of English and Fiction Writing, and that his tenure and promotion were almost entirely dependent on the amount of fiction he could reliably produce and publish in the space of an ever-shrinking period of time. He stayed up late at night filling page after page with scenes from his childhood, adolescence, and young adulthood, all of which were preoccupied with the illumination of what he had come to see as the towering genius of his older brother, who had not only an encyclopedic knowledge of silent film, surf music, John

Cassavetes, the Theater of Cruelty, early steam machines, Leslie Gore, eighteenth-century military percussion, and Evel Knievel, but also an uncanny ability to compose, arrange, perform, and produce at least five original songs per week, as well as a rare knack for writing one or two book-length manuscripts of poetry each season, and all of this in addition to his lifelong devotion to molding little animals in clay—mostly rabbits, squirrels, and ducks—all of which were depicted as intemperate, incontinent, chain-smoking, anemic, and debauched. The protagonist, after producing a book-length manuscript of thinly veiled autobiography that he knew he would never be able to share with his review committee at the college, never mind with a publisher, finally decided that life was not worth living. He climbed onto the roof of his two-story home and walked the perimeter, looking for the spot that could afford him the longest, deadliest leap. The north-facing side looked down onto the asphalt driveway, which was good, but he couldn't tell if the height would be enough to kill him, or to simply maim him. After standing and thinking for a bit, he decided that if he walked up to the peak of the roof's gable and then ran as fast as he could off of the edge, straight down into the asphalt, then he could probably build enough momentum to make a fatal leap. That is just what he did, and it worked.

He stopped scribbling on his legal pad. He couldn't think of a way for Simon to reenter the story, and it irked him. It was the first time in a long time that he had felt blocked. He stared at the empty dog bed on the floor next to his desk, and it suddenly struck him that there was no dog. Then, just as suddenly, that there was no dog bed, no cup of tea, no stone fireplace, no legal pad.

He stood up and stretched his stiff back. 🛡

Guess Who's Coming to Dinner

by Beth Gibbs

I am not a happy camper.

The brightly colored plastic flags adorning the used-car dealership on Willis Street flap smartly in the brisk November breeze. We drive past Conticello's Market and turn left on Clifford Drive. A familiar row of old two-story homes comes into view. Tension twists my neck muscles into knots of Gordian proportions.

Clay stops in front of a white house with dark-red trim. The bare hedges and naked maple tree in the front yard are stark evidence of winter's approach; the few leaves still clinging to its uppermost branches will probably fall before dark. I hope I'll fare better.

"Here you go, hon," Clay says. "Pick you up at six. Okay?"

"Clay, why wait till six?" My shoulders slump. My stomach churns. "Take me home now. Spare me the agony."

"Now, Virgie. We agreed to split up so we don't have to navigate two dinners and two families in the same afternoon."

He's right. This is a second marriage for both of us. Together, we've had five years of blended holidays in all sorts of configurations with in-laws, out-laws, children, and ex-spouses, but this is the first time I'll be alone with my family for a holiday since Clay and I got married. "I'll pick you up at six. Then we'll go home and lick each other's wounds, okay?" His eyebrows draw together and wriggle up and down—the "lust look." It never works. He looks too much like the Qantas Airlines koala bear.

"Okay." I kiss him and get out but linger with my hand on the door.

"Virgie."

"Okay!"

Clay gives me a wink. I reluctantly close the door and watch him drive off.

Growing up in a small New England factory town has its charms: friendly neighbors; a slow, leisurely pace; and no need to lock doors. It also has its demons, and I am about to have Thanksgiving dinner with several of them.

I walk up the steps and ring the bell. Mom opens the door.

"Hello, Virginia." She offers her cheek for my kiss but turns away before my lips reach it.

She heads down the hall to the kitchen. I follow, watching for signs of frailty. Everything from her fig-brown skin and pink warm-up suit to the frizzled grey company wig looks normal. If anything is missing, it's the mellowness that's supposed to come with age.

In the kitchen, Mom opens the oven to check on the turkey. Closing the door, she turns her head in my direction.

Her left eyebrow lifts. "So, how's everything with you?"

I want to tell her I'm fed up with corporate life, that I'd quit tomorrow but Clay and I are still helping the boys pay off their college loans. Instead, I say, "Okay, but I think I'm in a midlife crisis. I can't seem to—"

"Oh, I don't believe in this midlife crisis business, Virginia. I think one has to keep one's chin up and keep going. Most people give in to their feelings."

"Well, maybe, but I—"

"I've always kept a stiff upper lip. Why, your father never knew how devastated I was when he took our retirement money to bolster the liquor store." Mom moves to the counter and savagely tears lettuce into a salad. "That was a terrible blow. I had to scrimp and save for years to make up for it. Yes, indeedy, a stiff upper lip is what's needed."

I bite my lip.

"How's Fred?" Mom asks.

"He's fine. Mom."

"Why isn't he here?"

"He's hanging out with his friends today."

Her *humph* is followed by a *tsk* and then, "Does he have a steady girlfriend yet?"

"No, Ma. He and his friends still travel in packs. He's twenty-three. He's enjoying himself. I'm not going to worry about him until he turns thirty, and besides—"

"Thirty!" Her head shakes back and forth; the grey wig wobbles. "Lordy, his best years will be gone. He'll be too old to start a proper family. Honestly!"

I grit my teeth.

"And you know he never calls." She puts the salad bowl to one side. "I'm not going to give him anything for Christmas. As a matter of fact, I'm not going to give anybody anything for Christmas. It's such a hollow holiday now, all the focus on stuff instead of substance. The holiday lights and sales start the day after Halloween! It never used to be that way. It's not worth it."

She tops the salad with honey-roasted pecans. Mom's on a roll.

"And don't you get me anything, either. I have everything I need. Don't waste your money."

She brushes past me carrying a pan of Brown 'n Serve rolls.

"Can I do anything to help, Mom?"

"No, no, dear, you sit and relax." Cupboard doors slam. Pots and pans rattle.

"Mom, are you sure I can't help you with something?"

"Yes, yes, of course! That's what I said, isn't it? I can handle this. It's all set, really."

I watch her for a moment and then wander into the dining room to check on the table. The newly polished silverware gleams. The gold-rimmed china plates sit proudly on the table. The glassware sparkles. Handmade paper place cards grace each setting. All our names are there—except for two. Dad died ten years ago and Tamisha, my eight-year-old niece, died of a rare blood disease a year later.

Of course, Mom put my brother in Dad's chair at the head of the table. Tony, my pseudo-intellectual, Peter Pan brother has been married and divorced three times. He's always peddling some foolproof scheme for making big money. Last year at Easter, it was the smoothie bar on Main Street; by Mother's Day he wanted to open a consignment shop in the mall; and at the Fourth of July picnic, he pitched a food truck franchise he planned to run from his basement. Tony's schemes depend on money, time, and effort from everyone but him, but when they fail to materialize, it's anybody's fault but his.

Junior, Tony's fourteen-year-old son, is on his right. Junior's mom is in a psychiatric hospital. Junior blames Tony. Thandy, a musician and Tamisha's mom, is a few cards short of a full deck and Tamisha's death put her over the edge. Three months after the funereal, the police found her wandering stark naked down Main Street, playing "God Bless the Child" on her saxophone and proclaiming the second coming of Billie Holiday. Tony had no choice.

Next to Junior is Chuckie, whose spirit is as pure as they come. He's a bundle of undiluted four-year-old love-energy. His ability to remain unscathed by the vagaries of his father's life amazes me.

Adrienne's place card is on Mom's right. My younger sister lives her life as an empty journal waiting for an entry. The man she married wrote his life story all over her, a depressing saga of mental and emotional pain waiting for an ending. They're separated now but he's trying to romance her back. How someone like my sister managed to give birth to such a steady flame of sanity like Sydney is beyond me.

Sydney is seated between Adrienne and me, and on Mom's right is an extra setting with no place card. Huh? The doorbell rings.

"Get that, will you, Virginia?" comes Mom's voice from the kitchen. "It must be Adrienne and Sydney."

It is.

Back in the kitchen, after our "His" and "How've you beens," twelve-year-old Sydney scrunches her long-limbed plus-size body into a chair and glues her eyes to her smartphone. Adrienne, deep in her victim phase, is dressed head-to-toe in black. She drapes herself on a stool by the breakfast bar and vents.

"I don't know if I should take him back or divorce him, Mom. He keeps saying how sorry he is about cheating on me and he's been so sweet lately. He's even started taking Sydney out on father-daughter dates but I—"

"Take him back," Mom says, one hand on her hip and the other pointing a large wooden spoon at Adrienne. "I know what I'm talking about. A woman needs a man. It's God's law. Take him back and make Jordan change his ways."

"But, Mom—"

"No 'buts' about it. Take him back. Try some new recipes. Get out of those baggy black clothes. Put on some color, meet him at the door with a smile on your face and do whatever it takes to save your marriage."

Adrienne turns hopefully to me, but I can only manage a half-hearted smile and feel grateful that mom's righteous advice is no longer directed toward me.

Mom bustles. She bastes the turkey, checks the annual corn pudding, stirs the ever-present collard greens, and vehemently refuses all offers of help. It's not a good time to ask about the extra place setting.

The doorbell rings again. It's Tony and the boys. I get a wet quickie kiss from Chuckie before he makes a beeline to the kitchen to sniff out the treat his "Mu'dear" will have. Junior gives me a weak hug. Tony's eyes are unfocused; I can tell his thoughts are elsewhere, probably on his next big scheme. I give him cheek. Soon we're in the kitchen, Chuckie eating his treat, Junior and Sydney connected to their devices, and Adrienne in the middle of another complaint about Jordan. "I tried to talk to him about going to couple's counseling, but—"

"Counseling is a waste of time," says Mom. "It's all talk, talk, talk. And you know how I feel about airing private affairs in front of strangers. If you want your husband to act like the man you want him to be, you have to act like the wife he needs. Brush up on your womanly wiles." She grins and winks. "It always worked with your father."

Adrienne's face begins to crumple. Tony snatches the space between Mom's advice and Adrienne's oncoming tears to launch into his newest idea about flipping houses. "Listen, Virgie, it's foolproof. This town is bursting at the seams with run-down properties."

Mom watches Tony with her "no harm in indulging him" look. I steel myself for the pitch. "If you and Clay jump on this with me, we could be rolling in cash by next summer. I've got a list of prospects from the town clerk's office and all I need is . . ."

I tune him out. I'm drained, exhausted, done. It's all I can do to stand in the doorway and watch. I can't listen to another word, not from Tony, not from Adrienne, and not from Mom. Every holiday is the same. It's like we're caught in a time loop, living the same scene over and over. Nothing changes, not even the menu.

Mom samples the greens, smacks her lips, and looks at us with a twinkle in her eyes and says, "Guess who's coming to dinner?"

Intruder alert! Three pairs of black eyebrows shoot up, six brown eyes exchange quizzical glances, and three pair of shoulders hunch because Thanksgiving dinners at our house are traditionally limited to spouses and children. Spouses, not being blood relatives, are tolerated as social necessities; dates, lovers, and friends are actively discouraged or received with frosty politeness. Who could have wormed their way into Mom's good graces?

"Merle is coming up to visit her brother in Hyannis," Mom says. "She's going to stop and see us on the way."

Merle Fontaine of the Philadelphia Fontaines is Mom's first cousin. I've always liked Merle. She's flamboyant, outrageous, and classy. She has an infectiously upbeat attitude you can jump on and ride for miles. I cancel "intruder alert" and relax. With Merle here, Mom will be on her best behavior. Adrienne's "poor me" stories will cease, and Tony will try to sell Merle on his latest scheme instead of hounding me for money.

The doorbell rings a third time.

"It's Merle!" Mom sings out. She drops the spoon she'd been using to stir the greens. It clatters against the counter and hits the floor but she doesn't even notice. She wipes her hands on her apron and trots off to get the door.

Adrienne reaches down, picks up the spoon, and huffs as she puts it in the sink. The three of us exchange another set of meaningful glances. Mom never acts like that when one of us is at the door. For a moment we are united by a collective gloom. It isn't that Mom is uncaring. She's done the absolute best she could. She practically raised us by herself, holding down a full-time job as a salesclerk in a drugstore and managing the household alone. Dad was preoccupied with the liquor store and his golf game. Mom ran tired for years. We all knew what the deal was, and we all bear the scars. Tony's irresponsible, Adrienne is a doormat, and I'm an obsessive overachiever.

Two sets of footsteps trip lightly down the hall to the kitchen. We pull out our company smiles to momentarily eclipse the sadness.

Merle doesn't walk into a room; she sweeps in. Tall, thin, and willowy. With a swift motion of one manicured hand, her mink coat leaves her shoulders, traces a graceful arc through the air and lands on the stool next to Adrienne. Merle is wearing her signature color, cream, in the form of a lightweight wool pantsuit that clings to slender curves. Her hair, colored a deep mahogany brown, is swept up into a classic ponytail and the sparkle of her expensive jewelry pales before the twenty-four-carat joy in her eyes.

Her hugs, unlike those of my nuclear family, are close, tight, and warm.

Mom is beaming. Adrienne absentmindedly strokes Merle's coat with a faraway look in her eyes. Tony gives off vibes like a mountain lion ready to stalk newly spotted prey.

I cloak myself in forbearance and hope it will sustain me through the afternoon.

A few minutes later, dinner is ready. We sit in our designated seats. Tony says grace, and Mom fills our plates from steaming bowls and platters then passes them down the table. The kids dig in immediately. Merle's face is animated. Her hands fly through the air, and she tosses her words in our direction.

"Now, darlings," she says, "tell me what you've been up to. I'm dying to hear!"

Adrienne raises her head from her chest, gives Merle the 411 on Jordan and with a question mark in her eyes asks, "Merle, what do you think about divorce?"

Uh-oh. Out of the corner of my eye, I see Tony's forkful of greens stop halfway to his mouth. I follow his gaze and see Mom's eyebrows meet in the middle of a sudden but short-lived frown. Our baby sister has just violated Mom's rule about airing dirty laundry.

Merle clucks her tongue. "Divorce is a funny thing, dear. It comes down to what you get and what they get to keep." She reaches across the table to cover Adrienne's hand with hers. "Now, here's the tricky part: what they must never get or keep is your self-respect." She winks. "Sounds to me like you best leave him lay where the good Lord flung him and get on with your life!"

I watch Adrienne sit up a little straighter in her chair. There is a firm set to her shoulders, but she looks Mom's way as if searching for approval of Merle's advice. Mom's smile does not reach her eyes as she says, "Marriage vows are sacred. The Bible says 'Til death do us part.'"

"Things change, Martha," Merle says softly.

"Not all things," Mom replies.

Tony jumps into the silence that follows. "I'm working on a business proposition to flip houses," he tells Merle. She turns to smile at him. Mom's eye twitches.

"It's foolproof. Run-down houses around here are a dime a dozen. They're crying out for someone to buy 'em cheap, fix 'em up, and sell 'em at a profit. I'm looking for investors." I watch him pause to see how his pitch lands before moving in for the ask I know is coming. Tony is so predictable; this would be high comedy if it weren't so pathetic.

Merle calmly points out the positives—the certainty of making money if he does most of the work himself—and the negatives, like understanding that older homes often have serious code violations that will be expensive to fix.

Mom silently watches their exchange. I'm waiting for Tony to ask Merle for money. He doesn't. The smile on his lips is the first I've seen all day. He starts taking notes on his smartphone. He looks like a prize dog winning best of show.

"Excuse me," says Adrienne, getting up from the table. The look on her face tells me she's going to the bathroom for a private cry. I know she's unhappy but she needs to suck it up, make a decision about Jordan one way or the other, and spare us the drama. I didn't drag my friends and family through a never-ending story when I divorced Lenny.

Sydney, Junior, and Chuckie sit mesmerized by Merle's glitter, chatter, and charisma. She speaks to them on their level, no "my, how you've grown" stuff. She asks them about school, what they do in their spare time, and who their friends are. She pays attention to their answers. I'm surprised to learn that Sydney made the honor roll and plans to try out for the debate team. Junior's face relaxes as he tells Merle about his heavy metal band. They call themselves the Last Wave. Junior plays the drums. I did not know that. Chuckie tells Merle about his chess video game and how his favorite piece is the knight, "'Cause it looks like a horsey."

Eventually, even Mom's smile melts from Jack Frost winter to warm summer sunny as she and Merle crack up over silly stuff they did as teenagers: sneaking cigarettes behind Uncle Bob's garage and playing spin the bottle with their male cousins in the basement during family reunions. "And," says Merle with a chuckle, "that one time we got wasted on bourbon from Aunt Mary's secret stash."

Mom listens to every word, unlike the constant interruptions I get when I try to tell her what's going on in my life. Adrienne pats Sydney's shoulder on the way to her seat. I glance over and can almost see wheels turning in her mind. I wonder if she's made a decision.

By the time Merle asks me about my life, the energy in the room is as light and airy as the whipped cream on Mom's pumpkin pie. I hear myself telling Merle about my troubles but my mind has moved beyond my midlife muddle to settle on what's happening in this room right now. Merle seems completely unaware of her effect. She's getting everything I want to get from my family but can't.

My eyes watch while my mind calculates and questions, "the paralysis of analysis," as Clay puts it. The usual family drama is nonexistent—no interruptions or unsolicited advice. No bickering. How is this happening? Why is it happening? And most of all, why can't it happen when it's just us?

With my mouth full of stuffing and gravy, I suddenly know. Merle isn't trying to get anything. She isn't trying to fix our problems or change us. She is simply giving each of us her full attention and making thoughtful suggestions instead of telling us what we "should" do. Mom doesn't do that, I don't think Adrienne and Tony are capable of doing that, and as much as I hate to admit it, I don't do that either! My heart sinks. I put my fork down and sit stock still as the hard truth hits full force. I've got as many "oughts," "shoulds," and critiques as Mom does! The only difference is, she says hers out loud. Mine are silent and just as deadly. *Oh, my God. I'm one of the demons I've been complaining about!*

I'm surprised to feel shame. Shame for the mental put-downs and cynicism for dismissing Tony and his schemes before hearing him out or considering their potential; shame for tuning out Adrienne and her struggles without offering help, a listening ear or a shoulder to cry on; and shame for not paying more attention to Sydney, Junior, and Chuckie.

Mom starts to clear the dishes. Adrienne and I jump up to help. In the kitchen we pour juice for the kids and make tea and coffee for us. I catch Adrienne's eye and smile.

Back at the table I wonder what would happen if I listen, really listen to Mom's stories of stoic perseverance? What would happen if I really listen to Adrienne's "poor me" stories instead of thinking, *Oh, God, here comes another one*? What would happen if I took a more active interest in what my niece and nephews are doing with their lives? What would happen if I really listened to Tony and hear his pain? Maybe nothing, maybe everything, but it might be worth a try.

I feel a rush of love for my slightly dysfunctional, but very normal, family. It fills me up and tunes me in, at least for this moment. I give thanks for the insight. It seems an appropriate thing to do on this day.

An hour later, amid hugs and goodbyes, Merle heads off to Cape Cod, leaving behind the scent of her perfume and seeds for healthy new growth in the bonds between my family and me.

At 6:00 sharp, Clay arrives to rescue me, except I no longer feel the need to be rescued. He notices the smile on my face as we walk to the car.

"What's up, cupcake?"

I tuck my arm through his as we walk.

"Clay," I say, hugging my new feelings close to my heart, "guess who came to dinner?"

Sonder

by Meghan Evans

January 2020

17

My husband is so sick he sits up for seven nights in a row struggling to breathe. Then, trying to get to the bathroom, he stops breathing and collapses in the hall.

February 2020

310

Whispers roll in like fog. A virus has escaped a lab. A virus has incubated in a pig, a bat, a marketplace. The floor was wet, and people were breathing. A woman on the news warns, "Be prepared for significant disruptions to daily life."

The news flickers red and white in our dark living room and, yes, I am living, but sitting on the couch alone after he is dead, feeling the lights break and break over me is just senses firing. The television lights buck and buzz. Disruption is an optimistic word for the end of the life my husband and I were building. Disruption promises the ability to rebuild.

But I keep breathing, arriving at work, and going home, and he keeps not hugging me when I walk through the door. I'm a bag of sensory perceptions with touch crossed off the list.

I avoid the hallway where he died. Every moment is red and white flashing lights, shouting a message I can't hear.

March 2020

3,053

The cause of the rising death toll has a name. My freshmen class giggles, tastes it on their tongues experimentally, like the beer at their first high school parties. Coronavirus. One student says, "It's not affecting kids. I hope every teacher gets it and school shuts down." "That's not kind," I say. "You don't mean that." He grins, shapes the pointed hair of the Goku he is drawing. "I do. I hope every single adult dies." The novel we're reading slips from my hands. The rest of my class gets excited, imagining their homework-free futures; everyone except L—, whose parents are already dead.

Clorox disinfectant wipes. Grocery-store brand disinfectant wipes. Pasta. Baby formula. Every single box of Twinkies, gone. Two women hiss over possession of the last four-pack of toilet paper in the store, both squeezing their hands on the plastic, levitating it in mid-air, faces so close they could kiss. They don't pretend civility as I walk by pushing my cart—six sleeves of bagels and nothing else. Taste is crossed out, too. I'm just eating to stay alive, though I don't want to be anymore. It's confusing, to lose your partner and feel that cleaving, but not die from it. He is dead, and I'm standing in the grocery store, everyone fighting each other instead of the virus, surrounded by empty shelves like arms thrown wide in surrender.

April 2020

50,646

Teachers are superheroes. Teachers are miracle workers. They create and build online classrooms overnight. They show up in their students' driveways to teach music and math. They are spending their own money to keep students engaged. Colorful letters and supplies arrive in kids' mailboxes. The nation gasps. Have teachers always gone above and beyond like this? Educators have shown such love and dedication to their students that it flickers over me on the couch, newsworthy. I've been recording myself reading our books aloud, so students who struggle on the page can listen instead. I read into the computer's microphone each day after class until I'm exhausted, hating the grief I hear in my voice, trying not to remember all the times that going above and beyond for my students meant dipping into our savings for a vacation to Australia that we never went on, or meant my husband putting a plate in front of me at my desk, and eating his dinner in front of the television.

The television flinches and wobbles light at me from my dark corner on the couch, a bagel gone cold on a napkin in my lap. Protesters in Michigan want to work. Or they want everyone to see their guns. Or they want the nation to believe that Governor Whitmer's stay-at-home order aligns her policies with Hitler's, who they usually idolize, but not today! They do not want to social distance. They do not want to wear masks. It's not fair! They can't breathe in those damn masks.

May 2020

246,982

In Minneapolis, George Floyd can't breathe, and then he is murdered.

Physical touch is forbidden in this lockdown; when we touch, we kill.

I've been writing events and feelings down—my writing group said it might help me cope. They've watched me on their computer cameras gulping shallow bird breaths—trying to keep my racing heart beating into the next second, and the next, even though my husband is not in any of them—as we critique each other's work.

I haven't been able to catch my breath since his death. COVID squeezed out my husband's breath, and a police officer knelt on a man's neck and suffocated him. Yet, the news flicks images at me of people who complain masks restrict deep breathing, makes it seem like half the people in this country believe they will never, could never, be struggling to breathe.

Portland, Oregon catches fire. The keening blaze sucks up all the oxygen for miles, lighting torches in cities across the nation. In Hartford, Connecticut, my seniors lean toward their computer cameras, say they'll participate in the marches, waving their masks like flags. One student says, "Miss, I'm too afraid to go outside. Will you march with us? Like, in case you need to shield us?" "Of course," I say. Because I am a teacher. Because I am a human being. Because we are fighting each other unendingly and we are not fighting the virus and how is this still happening? Because if I really want to die, then all I have to be is what parents and administration across this country expect me to be: a teacher, shielding her students, waiting for a bullet.

My principal has received a complaint from a parent. Why am I reading so slowly in those recordings? It takes forever to listen to them! No one is interested in some useless Trojan War. I would stop wasting everyone's time if I just summarized the important parts of each chapter. The principal signs his email, "You're lucky to have a job in this economy so please do that job."

June 2020

397,186

I drop a bundle of letters into the mailbox outside the Newington post office. It's not my town, but I've gotten my hands on an N95 mask and so I've driven here for something to do. Each week I write to all the widowed women in my family, in my husband's family, living alone through the pandemic. There isn't much to say. I'm not baking bread, or practicing any self-care or workout routines, or becoming TikTok famous. I write about the birds in my neighborhood. I try to be funny. I share my observation that all that chirping just sounds like a chorus of "Shit! Shit! Shit!" The world is such a dumpster fire that even the birds have written a song about it.

Friends praise me for writing the letters, assuming I'm doing my part to support the flailing USPS. The truth is I'm so lonely that even my nightmares are just quivering versions of the silence in my house, sound crossed off too. There have been weeks when I don't speak a word out loud until Thursday night when I sign on to meet with my writing group. Whether I wake from the nightmares or not, I get out of bed on my husband's side and go into the silent hall, but I always make it to the bathroom, my lungs working just fine.

A man emerges from the post office, maskless. I step to the far edge of the sidewalk, and he clocks my movement instantly. "You scared I'm gonna give you COVID?" he barks. Before I can speak, he leans forward and coughs on me. "Better go get a rapid test, you fucking snowflake bitch." Then he climbs into a pickup truck with a bumper sticker that reads 'Kill Governor Lamont' with a little stick figure man swinging from what I assume is the Connecticut Charter Oak.

The birds sing, "Shit, shit, shit."

July 2020

539,962

Congressmen John Lewis dies. As I watch his casket move into South-View Cemetery, I remember his body, bent in pain over the death of his wife, eight long years ago. My body recognizes the shape of his body then, a grieving spouse. We bent toward the broken earth in exactly the same way, while my mind slipped off into the nightmare hallway.

I hear my husband's voice in every news interview with COVID patients and their families.

One man, still in the hospital but off the respirator, his eyes spectral, his blue gown stained with something yellow, implores us. "This is the sickest I've ever been." His wife and two daughters cry outside in the parking lot clutching an iPad. They have not seen him in person in three months.

Those are the words my husband spoke. "This is the sickest I've ever been." At the hospital they gave him an IV drip and told him it was a nasty flu, he needed to go home and rest.

"We can learn from the Spanish flu. Please don't become lax because the weather is nice. We must adhere to CDC guidelines," my local news anchor pleads. Black and white images of masked men and women in 1919 spark on the screen, one wearing a sign around his neck which reads, "Wear a mask or go to jail." Then, in 2020 color, footage of packed beaches and restaurants, the water a forgiving blue as bodies bend into graceful dives and disappear beneath the waves.

August 2020

711,849

Teachers are lazy. Teachers are selfish. They don't want to go back to school because they don't actually care about children. It's the teachers' responsibility to watch the kids while everyone else does the real work of recovering our economy. They aren't even considering the needs of parents! They whine about insufficient PPE, but kids are probably not carriers, and probably won't cause super-spreader events, which will likely be proven by returning to school!

Red school buildings glow in my dark living room.

We do this to each other: expect strangers to die so death never reaches us. I am not the Achilles I teach my students about, storming around Troy hoping to catch a stray arrow and join my beloved Patroclus in the underworld. I want what my husband wanted: to live.

I quit my job.

My school denies me unemployment. When I appeal, the argument their lawyer propounds is that I don't deserve it, because I didn't tell my principal why I was quitting. He agrees it was his right to know; I've really hurt his feelings. The school wins.

September 2020

889,326

California's summer wildfires turn into autumn wildfires, the writhing reds and oranges like anguished heart muscles, like nightmare versions of the foliage I'm anticipating in New England.

This is the first autumn foliage since I was four years old that I'm seeing without the corresponding return to school. It's possible I can become a leaf, detached not only from the trunk of my former life, but from the rotting branch of my former school. I am thirty-five years old, and since I'm alive, I have to start again. I must plant new seeds. I must force my way down that nightmare hallway in the flickering light and change the lightbulb.

Ruth Bader Ginsburg lives and lives and lives and then she dies. In death, she becomes the first woman and first Jewish person to lie in state at the Capitol. It's not clear behind people's masks, who's grimacing and who is smiling.

October 2020

1,043,413

The internet quips, "We can't say 'avoid it like the plague' anymore, since I guess no one avoids the plague."

Parents of 545 children separated at the US-Mexico border can't be found. The number of anti-Asian hate crimes rises across the country as the President slurs the phrase "China-virus" over and over on television. I want to feel love. I sleep on the floor in the hall on Halloween night to observe Samhain. My husband's ghost never wanders through the veil or presses his lips close to its gossamer to whisper in his kind voice. But all-night shadows dart from the window to the staircase. There are so many people who act on the belief that if love isn't visible, it doesn't exist.

November 2020

1,220,944

Biden and Harris are elected, making history, making the hope that we can learn to be good to each other possible. I write in my notebook: something does come next. One flickering light at the end of the hallway in my brain steadies, and in this nightmare life, it feels like one, small, safe space.

The Department of Labor contacts me. It seems I was allowed to receive unemployment after all. That sad principal was so convincing, but siding with the school turns out to have been illegal. Mindy on the phone tells me she sees this all the time, teachers denied automatically because the DOL assumes they're scamming unemployment during summer vacation. She's not supposed to, but she reviews as many former-teacher applications as possible. Her mother and sister were teachers. They both died this year, but she thinks they'd be proud of her vigilante work. She says she's trying to shine one little light into one little corner. I tell her I am proud of her and so grateful, and that the grief in my heart recognizes the grief in hers. We cry on the phone together.

December 2020

1,504,013

I haven't touched another person in almost a year when vaccines are approved in the U.S. Essential workers may finally feel a sliver of safety and a needle of hope. Nurses and doctors lean away from microphones. One doctor concedes, if she had any tears left, she might cry happy ones.

I have cried every single day for eleven months. Millions of people can say the same—all these humans being humans—but we can't meet or even trust each other, because nothing is getting better.

I don't know how to carry the weight of my husband's life into the future. I can't be him and myself. I don't know how to feel stronger.

January 2021

1,860,635

Rioters storm the capitol. They're loud and angry and violent. They didn't get what they wanted! It's not fair to be forced to live with an outcome you don't want!

Biden and Harris take office. I scroll through countless pictures that parents have posted of their little girls, sitting on carpets, transfixed by television images as Kamala Harris is sworn in. The images are surreal, in beauty, in power, in how long it's taken to get here.

And here we are, nearly a year into the pandemic. The jokes are about how long this year has taken. At least five years, minimum.

Husband, for a year I have been talking about you, when all I want to do is talk to you.

February 2021

?,???,???

I show this piece to my writing group and N—says, "It's dark. You need something funny. Like, put in Twinkies. You know, because it's the apocalypse." G— says, "It feels like you're leading up to something, but then, you don't. Where's the moral? How does it end? When does she finally get angry at one of these jerks?"

He gives me my first genuine laugh since 2020. "Angry? Who do you think she is? A man?" He raises his eyebrow in his diagonal box. "A woman's anger creates consequences for herself."

I have no moral and no moral high ground. My husband's life was leading to an adventure in Australia, growing old with me, a million moments of laughter, and then, it narrowed in our hallway and ended.

I have been angry at everyone.

All these human beings are dead. That will never end.

?

?,???,???

How will people tell the story of 2020 in ten years? Thirty? Who killed who? Can we ever forgive each other for all we refused to learn?

My husband died on the floor in our hallway, and I can't write about the alarm waking me in the steady light of dawn, about shuffling toward the bathroom.

Maybe if I had heard him. If I was more aware of what was happening around me. Maybe if I had woken up.

The light is flickering. Morning is too late. Wake up. 🛡

The Good Samaritan:
An Excerpt from *Burning Candles*

by Raouf Mama

Carima got to Kadia shortly before seven, as the little town awoke from sleep, and the sights and sounds of human activity gradually reestablished their dominion everywhere. Here a woman carrying an enormous basket overflowing with loaves of bread hawked her goods with a voice sweet as music, "Hot bread for sale, folks! Crunchy, tasty bread for sale!" A little further away a man riding an old rickety bicycle waved to a pedestrian in greeting. On either side of the street, people hurried by.

Footsore and travel stained, Carima sat on an old wooden bench next to a convenience store to rest and figure out what to do next. She thought back to her friend, Adiza, whose high-pitched voice and quiet humor she suddenly missed even more than she had as she took her first steps into the starlit night, homeless and forlorn, on her flight into the unknown long ago. She thought of Papa, of what he must have felt and said and done when he'd awakened to find her gone. She imagined what must have been his frenzied search—alongside Mama Fital and their incredulous neighbors—through bushes, side streets, and sheds. Adiza would have been among the searchers, Carima decided; in her mind's eye she could see her dumbstruck and robbed of the power of motion a moment upon hearing the news, then joining the search as she channeled her sorrow and her anger into action.

Carima wasn't sure she would ever see any of them again— nor was she sure of what she would say to them if she did.

Still, she chuckled at the thought of encountering them as she was—hair cropped short and no earrings, wearing tight-fitting blue jeans and a bottle-green shirt Papa had long discarded—and taking off her disguise as a boy to reveal her identity to them. She could imagine the expression of shock and bewilderment on Fital's goofy face.

It was then that Carima caught sight of the man. Of noble bearing, he was robed in white, and slung over his shoulder was a brightly colored bag made of synthetic material. His bushy beard was flecked with silver. The man looked left and then right as he waited at an intersection. Then he fired a glance towards Carima, or so she thought, before crossing. A shiver ran down her spine; instinctively, she averted her gaze, though she didn't want to. She wanted to watch this man, wanted to see where he was going.

In fact, she needed to.

When she looked again, the man had disappeared. It wasn't like she'd seen him before; he'd been a total stranger. Even still, she found herself springing to her feet as if her body had been programmed to do it from afar. Carima looked up and down the tree-lined street, frowning in concentration. Then, she snatched up her bag and hurried past a fat little boy who stood and stared after her a moment before going back to sweeping the dry and dusty patch of ground in front of his father's barbershop.

As Carima rushed helter-skelter along the street in pursuit of a total stranger to whom she felt a strange connection, a stranger who seemed to be playing cat and mouse with her, a voice spoke to her and said:

Find that man at all costs. He will be to you a better father than you have ever known.

Carima slowed her stride almost to a stop and pondered the mysterious voice a moment, oscillating between faith and doubt.

Then she quickened her pace anew in the direction she hoped the man had gone.

The sun was getting hotter and hotter as it rose ever higher in the sky, and Carima was covered in sweat and winded by her fruitless pursuit. The noise of traffic and a medley of voices calling, joking, cajoling, singing, remonstrating, or pleading filled her ears while the acrid smell of engine fumes, comingled with the aromas of fresh-baked bread and spicy food, tickled her nostrils. Carima looked right, left, and all around as she hurried along, scrutinizing any face that bore the slightest resemblance to the one she was after, but the face she sought was as elusive as a mirage.

Find that man at all costs. He will be a better father than you have ever known, the mysterious voice urged again.

Carima reached a juncture and saw to her right a handful of young men dressed in blue overalls, sporting construction workers' hard hats, clustered around a tall, fine-featured food vendor serving them food with one hand and collecting fees with the other. A sweet smile disclosed a row of shiny baby teeth now and then in response to the men's bawdy jokes and occasional accusations:

"Hey, Silas and I paid you the same, why is his portion twice as big as mine?" one voice cried shrilly. "Good looks are not part of the deal here, are they?"

"Wait a minute!" another voice called out with a laugh. "You and that fellow over here are from the same village I know, but I am much older than he and have been your client for much longer. Did you never get the message in that popular song, 'Age Before Beauty,' my dear?"

A delicious smell of rice and beans made Carima's stomach growl as she surveyed the scene a moment. She was faint with hunger and thirst, but she knew she couldn't tarry and, begrudgingly, moved along.

As she neared the marketplace, the squeals and intermittent laughter of a small crowd drew her attention. A moment later, she found herself at the edge of the gathering. Still moving as if controlled by another, she squeezed between two women, the fabric of their dresses scratching against her arms, and found—at *last*—the man she'd been looking for.

He was sitting on a bench and smiling, while all around him, a motley assortment of people stood as though transfixed.

"Babouka, you are one of a kind! I love your stories!" someone exclaimed. Then the speaker stepped forward, made a little bow, and flung a fistful of coins into a bowl at Babouka's feet. A few others in the crowd followed suit, and the tinkling of coins filled the air like music.

"Give us a riddle, Babouka!" another voice rang out. This time, it was a boy no older than ten, with big roving eyes that, for a moment, happened to meet Carima's. Instead of the voice filling her mind and urging her onward, something else inside of her head now pulled her backwards to "The Abode on The Far Side" where she, her best friend Christopher, their mentor Pierre, Lazarus, and a bunch of other homeless children had lived for five years. But it didn't pull her back to the night she and Christopher first arrived at "The Abode on The Far Side," and Pierre introduced them to Lazarus and the other homeless kids who welcomed them with lights in their eyes. Instead, it took her to the night before. To the mahogany table at the police station where Christopher's lifeless body had been laid. To the smashing of boots against wood, the snapping of metal hinges, and the crack of the door against the wall at the start of the police raid on "The Abode on The Far Side" two hours earlier.

"Lazarus!" Carima muttered under her breath, recovering herself, "he reminds me so of Lazarus!"

But she looked away so as not to embarrass the boy—especially because Babouka had begun to speak.

"I am more precious than gold and rubies. I cannot be bought or sold, and the more you give me away, the more I increase. What am I?"

A chorus of voices rose, proposing various things, but none did Babouka find satisfactory.

"I am Love," he said at last, his eyes gleaming.

The crowd cheered, asking for more.

"Time has flown, and I must go home," he responded. "But I will give you one to ponder until we meet again tomorrow. I am powerful. I visit people all the time, and I often change their lives forever. What am I?"

As people drifted away, Babouka emptied the contents of the bowl into one of his pockets. Dropping the bowl in his bag, he brought out a plastic bag containing a mango. He sniffed it and grimaced before heading for a nearby garbage can.

Carima held her breath, eyes shut. She needed to go and speak to this man—she'd chased him all the way across town—but what was she supposed to say? Why had she even followed him in the first place? Because this voice had told her to? Why hadn't it also told her what to say to him when she found him? When she reopened her eyes—to make sure she hadn't lost the man again—Babouka was standing a few steps away.

"Why are you crying, friend?" he asked in a voice smooth as velvet. "What ails you?"

She hadn't realized she'd started crying. Hadn't felt it happen. "What?" she said numbly.

"What ails you?" Babouka repeated.

How could Carima possibly tell a total stranger about the hunger burning her stomach and the greater hunger of her need, however strongly she may feel drawn to that man?

No, she needed time to think things through, to get to know him a little better.

"What is the matter, my child . . . Why are you crying?" Babouka said once more, drawing a little closer.

"I don't know," Carima replied, her tears flowing fast. "I can't . . . I can't tell you."

"That's all right," Babouka said. "That's quite all right. You don't have to explain."

The voice that had spoken to her shortly after she laid eyes on Babouka sounded in her ear once again. *He will be a better father than you have ever known.*

"I am Carima," Carima said, and she held out her hand—again without truly knowing why or meaning to do it.

The moment Babouka had first laid eyes on Carima, he had known that he was in the presence, not of a boy as appearance proclaimed, but of a girl in disguise. His sharp eye and penetrating wit had spotted the deception, but he held his peace, for it was an article of faith with him that the heart has reasons of its own that reason itself knows nothing about. Still, the girl looked haggard, was dirty and sweaty and shaking a little at the knees. He couldn't just leave her there in the middle of the marketplace.

"Be careful here, old man," he cautioned himself as he considered how best to win the child's trust. "The road to hell is paved with good intentions. As you well know." Indeed, Babouka remembered his own arrival in Kadia, a total stranger in need of a place to stay, desperate to turn over a new leaf and keep his past a secret. Well did he remember the kindness and gentle manner of the Islamic priest, Malik by name, who took him in for the night and helped him purchase at a bargain price the place he now called home. He shuddered to think how he would have reacted if Malik had harassed him with questions about his hometown, his identity, his motives for coming to Kadia, and his past, or had appeared too eager or too forward. The gratitude he felt then and still felt all those years later, long after Malik had gone to his Maker, filled his heart with empathy for Carima. He would never have needed to escape to Kadia in the first place if things hadn't gone the way they'd gone, and so while he wondered what could have made the child disguise herself as a boy, he decided to leave it be. Instead, Babouka reached out and took her hand and said, "Come with me. I will show you where I live. You can stay with me if you want."

Carima's vague fear of the unknown and her residual mistrust of strangers faded in an instant, and she felt no surprise and had no hesitation—only joy and thanksgiving—when her body again operated independently of her conscious will and she nodded along to Babouka's offer.

For his part, Babouka felt something like a mild electric shock go through him when their hands touched. He made nothing of it, however, dismissing it as a freakish manifestation of his own overexcitement. Only later, in the radiant light of hindsight, did he see it as an early sign of Carima's supernatural power and the miraculous cure for the arthritis that had come to him with the season of old age.

***

Babouka's house lay at the edge of town, a simple but spacious mud-wall structure thatched with reeds and hidden apart from the urban sprawl like an oasis nestling in the far reaches of a desert.

"Make yourself at home," Babouka said with a broad smile.

A feeling of joy stirred in Carima's breast as Babouka pointed to a library overflowing with books, a little bathroom with a sink topped by a mirror, and a tiny sitting room / dining room. At one end of the house was Babouka's bedroom wherein a lantern burned in broad daylight, and at the other end was a guest room of comparable size, which Babouka said was to be her own.

After Babouka excused himself and went out to give her privacy, Carima gazed around her new room, running her fingers along the unpainted walls, checking the closet as well as the full-length mirror inside it, and pacing up and down in great excitement. She had lost her cozy little room at "The Abode on The Far Side" forever, but she had found this, and it was cozier and more beautiful than words could say!

When she came out to tell Babouka how much she loved his house and how grateful she was for his kindness, she found that Babouka had put out food and drink for her, a simple lunch consisting of smoked-fish stew and boiled plantains.

"Who could this man be, and what is the secret source of so much kindness and such warm hospitality toward me, whom he has just met and knows nothing about?" Carima wondered as she tossed and turned on her mat in search of sleep following her long journey.

She felt such an outpouring of gratitude toward her host that her stomach lurched at the thought of keeping him in the dark about her true identity and her quest a moment longer. The story of her life, from her flight from home disguised as a boy to her departure from Lego the night before; what a relief it would be to unburden herself, make a clean breast of it, and, if the voice in her head was to be believed, embrace life here as Babouka's adopted daughter! That, surely, would be the sensible thing to do!

And yet, deep in her heart, she felt a tug of caution, an instinctive fear of speaking out of turn and rushing to bare her soul and reveal that which she had better conceal. The more she debated within herself the rights and wrongs of secrecy and transparency, the more muddled she felt until, mercifully, she closed her eyes in sleep at last. Or, at least, that's what was about to happen—until she was pulled all the way awake again by a melodious voice singing "What a Wonderful World," a song that had made every fiber in her body thrill and frolic with pleasure since the first time she'd heard it as a small child out in her parents' garden.

Carima listened, nodding in time to the music until it dawned on her that the voice was not that of some gifted singer who had come by the house to sing for his supper, but the voice of Babouka himself singing his heart out in a moment of leisure.

"God, he must have peace in his soul and love that passes all understanding to sing like that," Carima thought to herself. "Such beautiful, soul-lifting singing must flow out of a deep-seated reservoir of boundless love and goodwill toward all men."

"Is this," she asked the mysterious voice that had urged her to find Babouka, "is this why you sent me after him? Why you brought me here?" Was it to find someone who actually embodied the love they claimed to have for others? Someone who might actually help me because he wanted to—rather than because he felt obligated to? Unlike the others.

Unlike even Papa, the only father she had known until the moment she ran away from home. ◈

Not the Kiss

by Candace Barrington

Though not a man known for aesthetic discernment, still he surprised her the first time he opened the door. Looking past him, she beheld a proudly framed print of Klimt's "The Kiss." She had hoped for more. Maybe she wouldn't have been so disappointed if the poster had been displayed à la college dormitory: tacked to the wall, an edge or two torn, with visible creases. But someone—Him? Former girlfriend? Hippy earth goddess at the flea market?—had paid for an equally gaudy frame, all gold and kitschy. He heard her gasp and smiled.

For the next hour, they drank Chablis and ate chunks of cheddar on Triscuits. He tried to engage her in small talk, politely avoiding workplace chit-chat. His witty stories made her smile. The one about a nosy neighbor made her giggle. Yet she found herself stealing glimpses of the print. Is this how he imagined romance? The woman on her knees, her head twisted in his grasp?

More small talk. An amusing tale of over-ripened peaches. Another glimpse. What's wrong with that woman's right hand? Is she pushing him away? Is she even alive?

Enough small talk. Before the bottle was empty, she called it a night. He took her extended hand and shook it, suggesting dinner in a week or two. At his place downstairs. The repairs from the burst pipes should be completed by then.

"Maybe—"

A final glimpse.

"Do you play backgammon?"

Dream Police

by Anthony D'Aries

Laura found the place, made the call, and scheduled the pickup. The pickup. Like we were to leave Michelle in a bag at the end of our driveway. The woman on the phone told Laura she was doing the right thing. Laura told me we were doing the right thing. I'm still not sure.

I was on a flight to New York when they came for her. The agency had called some last-minute, urgent meeting—the only kind they ever call—so I had to be there. A few nights before, Michelle had come home drunk. Drunk is not the right word. Too cutesy, too much room for fun. Puking didn't even faze her. She sat up, opened her mouth, and everything inside poured down her shirt. No convulsing. No sound. By the time the ambulance arrived, she was barely breathing, her skin the color of bone.

When we brought her home, she made jokes in the car and sipped orange Gatorade, the hospital bracelet sliding up close to her elbow.

Laura yelled at her. She yelled in the car, in the driveway, through the kitchen, up the stairs, and continued to yell after Michelle slammed and locked her door. When Laura came back down, she was sweaty, her face flushed like she'd just gone for a long run. But there wasn't that gentleness, that peace in her eyes.

"How can you just sit there?" she wanted to know. "After what she did?"

I put my bowl of grapes on the coffee table. "We just got home. She's alive; that's the most important thing. Give her some time."

Laura walked into the other room. I reached for a grape but thought better of it, and listened to her rustle through some papers until she came back in and handed me a business card with sharp corners. At the bottom, a small logo: two hands cupping a sapling.

"Hillock Academy?"

Laura nodded. "Rebecca gave it to me at our last session. They take care of everything. Insurance'll cover it. Some of it, anyway."

My fingers curled around the card. "But what do they do?"

"They help, Don. They help parents who don't know what the fuck to do. They help kids—" She tried again. "They help kids before it's too late."

Before it's too late. I'd soon hear that phrase from social workers, counselors, every staff member at Hillock Academy. I'd read it in brochure after brochure, testimonials from other parents "just like us." But hearing Laura say it for the first time was like watching an actress audition for a role she didn't want.

***

The next day, Michelle came downstairs for breakfast.

"Hey," I said. "Casper the hungover ghost."

"Funny, Dad."

The plastic bottoms of her slippers *shushed* across the kitchen floor. She opened the cabinet.

"I think you can take that off now," I said, pointing to her bracelet.

She smiled and twirled it. "I don't know," she said. "It's a good look, don't you think?"

I took a big spoonful of cereal and chewed. "Very classy. And you'll never have to worry about forgetting your name."

She laughed, reached for the box, and shook some into her bowl. With the tips of her fingers, she put the flakes, one by one, into her mouth.

"You've been eating cereal the same way since you were three years old," I said.

"I was ahead of my time."

It was her cockiness that disturbed Laura the most. Michelle had that teenage-invincibility thing, and we'd never convince her otherwise. How could we? Alcohol poisoning, a trip to the ER, and the next day she's good as new. A little queasy, a little pale, but nothing some Gatorade and crappy TV couldn't fix.

I'd think about that breakfast for years. Michelle's pale skin, her raccoon eyes. Delicate as a porcelain ballerina with a crooked spine of Krazy Glue. How my fear mutated into stupid jokes. How I convinced myself that my silent love was a time-release drug that would slowly cure her. How I shouldn't have let Laura make that call.

But like I said, I was 30,000 feet in the air when the van came. I got the story later. Alex, Michelle's on-again-off-again boyfriend, thought it was a good idea to bring her and some of his buddies up to the water tower to "tweak" or "get ripped" or whatever scumbag, brain-dead way they put it these days. This was two days after she got home from the hospital. Laura thought she had her under house arrest, but Michelle is Superwoman. No window too small, no roof too high. Laura called the number on the card as soon as she realized Michelle was gone.

"I had to, Don," she said. "I didn't know what else to do."

I pictured a blacked-out van with a sliding door. The kind

that might park in an alleyway against the brick wall of a jewelry store while two bumbling cat burglars slide open the door and drill a hole through the wall. They crawl inside, yank trays of precious stones from display cases, dump them into drawstring canvas bags, and then disappear into the night.

By the time I landed in New York, Michelle was already on her way to Hillock Academy. She called me the next morning sobbing, her voice crackling through the phone.

"Two fucking meatheads in polo shirts kidnap you at three in the morning. How would you feel, Dad?"

***

A few days later, after Laura went to bed, I sat on the couch and reread the Hillock brochure. Glossy photos of an expansive green lawn stretching up to a seaside mansion. A low-angle shot from the beach: large, jagged rocks fortifying the foundation, wide bay windows reflecting the ocean. Photos of teenagers with their arms around each other, smiling, their clothes seemingly brand new like models from a catalogue. *Which one of these kids looks the happiest?* the ad team might've wondered. *Which one looks the least sick?*

And the tone, my god. That tone they use in these brochures—the same kind our copy team pumps out day after day. Sentences tailored to your weaknesses, your vulnerabilities. Hillock Academy features "clinically-intensive, evidence-based therapies" and "family support" and the "full continuum of care, from crisis intervention to aftercare planning." They provide a "safe environment" for teens. The brochure whispers like a mass card. *Let go and let Hillock.*

I finished my drink, laid down on the couch, and stared at our Christmas tree. Something about those little white lights, how they twinkled through the red and green ornaments like liquor bottles. My mother's glass angel balanced on top. Tell you the truth, I don't know how we pulled it together that year, but it was up, it was decorated, and that had to count for something.

***

Laura packed a cooler bag with plastic containers: homemade chicken noodle soup, meatloaf, mashed potatoes, and a tin of Christmas cookies. I walked back and forth between the car and the house. The first couple of trips were on purpose, but then I forgot my sunglasses, and then I forgot my cell phone. Without fail, I always end up in this ritual, this pacing between house and car. I don't even fight it anymore. This is just the way I leave the house. It's almost like when a dog walks in circles on the couch before settling in to sleep. I heard they do that because when they were wild, they stamped down the ground and flattened out a spot for their bed. Maybe my pacing is some displaced instinct, something that served my ancestors but is useless to me now.

"Do you think she needs more blankets? Or an extra pillow or something?" Laura asked.

"Couldn't hurt."

I went back inside and up to Michelle's room. I stood in the hallway for a moment, my hand on the doorknob. How many times had I stood in that exact position, waiting, listening? Listening for the crack of a beer, the burbling of a bong, or worse—heavy breathing. Now nothing. The door creaked open. This wasn't Michelle's bedroom anymore. It was a time capsule. A museum exhibit. *Teenage Bedroom, circa 2017*. Laura had already cleaned it since the pickup, and I couldn't remember the last time I'd seen the wood floor, or the bed made. Everything was dusted and polished: the tin tray of candles on her dresser, the small ceramic vases stuffed with drawing pencils on her desk, her bookshelves—mostly poetry and screenplays of her favorite movies. Lording over this obscenely clean room were her band posters: a pale, dark-eyed woman, half naked, reaching out; and serious tough guys in black knit hats and tank tops, tattoos curling up their chests and necks. I opened her closet, pulled down a spare blanket and with it came her middle school backpack, the dark-blue monogrammed JanSport. The white "M" was filled in with black ink. It looked deflated. I only ever saw it filled to capacity and strapped to her little body. Here, it seemed out of place, like a sneaker on the side of a highway. I hung it on the doorknob, shut the closet, and went back downstairs.

***

Whenever I see those movies or TV shows where a character steps into a parallel dimension and discovers an alternate version of himself, I think of parents' weekend at Hillock. On the surface, everything was fine. The lawn and hedges trimmed with military precision, the hallways sparkling, the coffee dispensers gleaming. "Welcome" tote bags with HILLOCK stamped on the front filled with two HILLOCK T-shirts, two HILLOCK water bottles, and a couple of HILLOCK pens and pads—not unlike the swag my team and I distribute to doctors' offices. Laura and I were both dressed up, though I wasn't sure why. Some of the other parents were too. Others wore baggy sweatshirts and jeans, or T-shirts and baseball hats. Those other men surveyed the building, and took note of the furniture and light fixtures. Those other men ran estimates in their head, their brain tissue like stacks of carbon paper, and the number they arrived at was the exact amount Hillock was going to drain from their paychecks every week. Those other men thought of driving a fist through the drywall and imagined a beam of light shining back, a peephole into the shadow world; the one we all wanted to be true, the one where we were gathered in the marble lobby of a prestigious college rather than the cavernous vestibule of a glorified halfway house.

In a glass case was some kind of wall of fame. Patients who

had gone on to do great things. Except they didn't call them "patients," they called them "guests." Like Michelle was *invited*, rather than thrown into a van and forced there. Were all the kids stolen in the middle of the night? Or did some of them have parents with enough guts to drive them there? So many of them looked oddly similar, like a portrait gallery of the Kennedys: neat brown hair, square jaws, triumphant gray-green eyes. They went on to start companies, travel the world, and raise families. Each bio offered an italicized testimonial with their parting words:

I thought my life was over when I first came to Hillock. Turns out, it was the opposite.

Hillock taught me how to have empathy, especially for myself.

Hillock is my second home.

The last one disturbed me the most. Your second home? What did Shaun Donohue mean by that? That he loved his time here so much it was equal to the home he was raised in? Or was his first home so miserable that Hillock didn't have much competition?

"Don?" Laura said. "Don. The tour's starting."

She grabbed my hand and led me back to the group. We reeked of coffee and sweat. All of us had a long drive. Nobody lived near Hillock.

At the front of the group was a tall, severely thin woman with a sharp nose and sharp cheekbones. She looked carved from stone.

"Good morning, parents," she said. "I am Mary Dalton, chief executive officer of Hillock Academy. On behalf of our staff and guests, welcome."

Silence.

"I always like to begin by saying you made the right decision. A decision no parent wants to make, of course. To be frank, I wish we lived in a world where Hillock was obsolete.

Unnecessary. Until then, we're here to help you and your child rebuild."

Laura leaned forward with her chin up like a houseplant basking in a slice of sunlight. My disgust surprised me. I felt the way I did on road trips decades ago when she slyly asked if I wanted McDonald's, knowing I'd give in as long as she asked first. And how I judged her even as I took my own greedy bites of a delicious, poisonous burger.

Mary Dalton led us down gleaming hallway after gleaming hallway: closed doors with gold plaques, a few associate directors, and nearly a dozen case workers. At the end of one hallway, a floor-to-ceiling, stained-glass window. A line of children holding hands and following a tall woman. Rays of sunlight beaming down on them. I got a closer look at the children's faces as we walked by. They weren't smiling, but they also weren't unhappy. Masks of serenity.

Down one of those hallways, behind one of those doors, was Michelle. Maybe lying on a thin mattress on a bed frame of scuffed wood. Maybe a matching desk, a marble notebook. Were they allowed to have pens? Were the rooms the same as the ones in the brochure? Or did they use a stage—a fake room much nicer and cleaner than the real dorms?

At the agency, we talk a lot about "perception." How consumers perceive us, how we perceive consumers. What I've learned over the past two decades is that the truth doesn't matter. It's what we *believe* to be true that's important. You're a health-conscious person and you're shopping for honey. One jar has a generic label, another is in a little burlap sack with a handwritten tag: "Local." Chances are you'll pay an extra few bucks for the local brand—even though it might not be any healthier or even closer to home than the generic. But that doesn't matter. You believe that it's better, so it's better. When you taste it, you feel better about yourself and feeling better about yourself makes the honey taste sweeter, purer. So I chose to believe that the room in the brochure was the room that Michelle was in.

Mary Dalton walked and talked while gesturing at the walls and ceiling, and pointing to the green lawn and snow-dusted pine trees in the distance. "Hillock offers around-the-clock support to over fifty guests in a state-of-the-art facility," she said, and we followed her like elementary school students. Single file. Inside voices.

***

We didn't sit down until lunch. A massive cafeteria. Each set of parents sat at a different table. Along the side, a row of stainless-steel, dome-topped serving trays. Something safe was inside: roasted potatoes and grilled chicken, maybe, or penne Bolognese. Servers stood behind the table; shiny spoons cocked in white-gloved hands.

"I'm too nervous to eat," Laura said.

I nodded and looked at the next table. One of the baseball hat dads was chowing down. Hunched over, shoveling, like a starved inmate. Who was I to judge? Maybe this wasn't his first rodeo. Maybe for some, having your kid taken away in the middle of the night and driven two states away was common. There must be—what would we call them?—repeat offenders. No, "frequent guests."

Somewhere above, a soft chime sounded, the doors opened, and Michelle walked in. Her Hello Kitty pajamas hung loosely around her waist, her upper half somewhere beneath an extra-large HILLOCK sweatshirt. Other kids flowed around her. I thought of kennels, of abandoned dogs lined up for viewing. She met our eyes. I decided the shape of her mouth was a smile.

"Hey, sweetie," I whispered, pulling her close.

"How are you, honey?" Laura asked.

Michelle looked confused. We stood for a moment, then sat down.

"Are you getting enough to eat?" Laura reached into the cooler bag.

"Please, Mom," Michelle said. "No food."

Laura clasped her hands in front of her.

"How are you feeling?" I asked.

Michelle shrugged. Some other families spoke in hushed voices. Some were silent. The servers waited.

"Do you get outside much?" Laura asked. "It's a beautiful property."

"Then why don't *you* live here, Ma?" Michelle laughed. "If it's so beautiful."

We sat in silence for who knows how long. Too long.

Some of the families got food and returned to their tables. Michelle looked around in the cooler bag. She pulled out the tin of Christmas cookies and stared at it for a few seconds. There was a hollow *ping* when she dropped it back into the bag. She took an apple instead.

"So," I said. "What are your days like? Are there activities or meetings? Classes or something?"

"Yeah," Michelle said. "So many meetings. Everyone in here is a total fuck up."

"You're not," Laura said.

"I didn't say I was. I said everyone else."

Laura sighed and looked at me. I held her stare for a moment, then turned away. Michelle took a slow, quiet bite of her apple.

It occurred to me: Taxicol. A new drug the agency was marketing. The one I'd been called in to New York to discuss the day the van took Michelle away. The commercial my boss said would bag us a Clio Health Award. A black-and-white clip of an angsty teenage girl slumped beside her untouched breakfast. A hand squeezes her shoulder, and the narrator describes the symptoms of depression and anxiety. And although we never see the girl taking Taxicol, we know from the way the colors brighten, the way she walks out the door smiling, the montage of bike rides and pizza parties and study sessions, that the drug is working. Then we see the girl as a young woman backing out of the driveway in her beat-up car filled with cardboard boxes and the parents standing on the stoop, the father's arm around the mother. They share a look that screams "WE DID THE RIGHT THING," and this is almost enough—almost—to ignore the narrator's quiet avalanche of side effects.

I wanted to stand up in the middle of this fake lunch, in this polished room that smelled vaguely of bleach. I wanted to scoop up Michelle and get her out of there, and if Laura wanted to come too, fine, but if not, we were leaving anyway. I'd quit my job and become an organic farmer or a carpenter. Maybe both. Build a new house on the edge of some woods. Michelle, freshly showered, her long, wet hair hanging down to the middle of her back, would stand poised in the field like a wild horse, lingering long enough for me to appreciate her strength before charging off into the trees.

Michelle laughed, as if she could hear my thoughts.

"Where were you, Dad? Mom had me fuckin' kidnapped. Where were you?"

***

On the ride home, we stopped at a gas station. Laura was hungry. She came back with a hot dog in a little paper coffin and a box of cherry cough drops.

"Remember these?" she asked, shaking the box.

"Oh, wow," I said. "I haven't seen those since I was a kid. We used to eat them like candy."

We pulled out of the gas station onto Route 2. The dark road ran straight for miles. Every other house or so shined like a miniature Las Vegas with red and green Christmas lights lining the gutters and windows, and wrapped around bushes and trees. One house turned the garage into Santa's workshop, complete with an assembly line of animatronic elves stiffly hammering wooden wagons and slack-jawed puppets. Then there was the latest trend that depressed the shit out of me, something Michelle and I made fun of any time we saw it: those lazy blow-up decorations. Big, bloated Santa Clauses and roly-poly Rudolphs, their electrical pumps whirring all night long.

There were dark houses, too. Ones that stood stark and silent. No lights. No blow-up Santa. Nothing glowing inside.

I wanted to ask Laura if she thought Michelle would be home for Christmas. I wanted to ask, but I knew the answer. I just wanted her to say it, so when I had to think about it night after night after night, the words would be in her voice, not mine. Our bodies pulsed against each other like opposite poles of a magnet.

Laura shook out two cough drops and offered me one. She put hers in her mouth and turned away. I crunched mine between my teeth, the red shards melting beneath my tongue. I could already feel it working. ◈

Contributors

Candace Barrington lives in New Haven, Connecticut, and teaches ancient, medieval, and contemporary global literature at Central Connecticut State University. She collaborates with authors, translators, and scholars on every continent (except Antarctica); this story began in an online writer's workshop that originated in Cyprus during the 2020-2021 pandemic lockdown.

Christine Beck is a poet and teacher of literature and creative writing. She holds a Masters of Fine Arts in Creative Writing. Christine Beck is a former Poet Laureate of West Hartford, CT. Her books of poetry include *Blinding Light* (Grayson Press), *I'm Dating Myself* (Dancing Girl Press), *Stirred, Not Shaken* (Five Oaks Press) and Beneath the Steps: a Writing Guide for 12-Step Recovery. Her website is www.ChristineBeck.net.

Chris Belden is the author of the novels *Shriver* and *Carry-on*, as well as the story collection *The Floating Lady of Lake Tawaba*.

Kethry Bentz's love of literature was first sparked when their mother plopped them down on their bedroom floor and read aloud the entire set of Magic Treehouse books. Raised in the rolling hills of northwest Connecticut, Kethry's logomania can only be rivaled by their love of all things nature. Hiking, studying bugs, and listening to the birds sing their unnamed songs are what brings them peace when they're not reading or writing.

Lary Bloom's books include *Sol LeWitt: A Life of Ideas, Letters From Nuremberg, The Test of Our Times, The Ignorant Maestro, The Writer Within,* and *Lary Bloom's Connecticut Notebook.* His plays: *Worth Avenue, Wild Black Yonder, A Woman of a Certain Age* (lyricist). His columns have appeared in the *New York Times, Hartford Courant,* and *Connecticut Magazine.* He lives in New Haven, teaches in the Yale Writers' Workshop, and is a freelance book editor.

Victoria Buitron is a writer and translator who hails from Ecuador and resides in Connecticut. She received an MFA in Creative Writing from Fairfield University. Her work has appeared or is forthcoming in *Lost Balloon, XRAY Lit Mag, Entropy, Bending Genres,* and other literary magazines. Her debut memoir-in-essays, *A Body Across Two Hemispheres,* is the 2021 Fairfield Book Prize winner and will be available in Spring 2022 by Woodhall Press.

David Cappella is the co-author of two books on the teaching of poetry: *Teaching the Art of Poetry* (Routledge) and *A Surge of Language* (Heinemann). He won the 2006 Bright Hill Press Poetry Chapbook Award. His poems have appeared nationally and internationally. His book *Gobbo: A Solitaire's Opera* will be published in Summer 2021 by Červená Barva Press and will be published as an Italian bi-lingual edition by *puntoacapo Editrice* in November 2021.

Holly Carignan lives in Connecticut with her three irresistible, pesty, entertaining cats. She has an old, unused MA in psychology and, more recently, a BS in biochemistry. When she is not slogging away in a hospital lab, she is home writing by computer light in the comfortable darkness of her messy house. She is a proud member of the Westport Writer's Workshop, and is forever indebted to them for their friendship and support.

Julie Choffel grew up in Austin, Texas, where she studied geography, ecology, and writing. Her poems have appeared in many journals, most recently in *New American Writing, Interim, Salamander, Western Humanities Review, and the Wallace Stevens Journal.* She is the author of *The Hello Delay* and *The Chicories,* a graduate of the MFA Program for Poets and Writers at UMass Amherst, and an adjunct professor of creative writing at the University of Connecticut.

Z'Jahniry Coleman is an eighth-grade student. Outside of writing, her main hobby is cosmetology (hair, nails and a little bit of makeup). She wrote the poem included in this anthology for a contest when she attended Greater Hartford Academy of the Arts Magnet Middle School. It was inspired by a scene from the Netflix show Ginny & Georgia.

Ken Cormier is the author of *Balance Act* and *The Tragedy in My Neighborhood.* He has released four collections of original music, and he makes radio fiction and documentary pieces, many of which have aired on public-radio affiliates around the US and on the BBC. He directs the Creative Writing Program at Quinnipiac University. More info at: thebenjysection.com/kencormier

Jason Courtmanche is Assistant Professor in Residence in English, Affiliate Faculty in Teacher Education, Director of the Connecticut Writing Project, and Assistant Coordinator of Early College Experience English at UConn. Recent publications have appeared in *English Journal, CT Literary Anthology, Professions, WPA, Deep Reading, Nathaniel Hawthorne Review, Resources for American Literary Study, Writers Who Teach, What Does It Mean To Be White In America?, What Is 'College-Level' Writing?,* and *Nathaniel Hawthorne in the College Classroom.*

Born and raised in New York City, Thomas Cowen lives in the beautiful town of Ridgefield, CT. He is an above-average sales engineer, retired amateur boxer, and barely serviceable hockey player. He has been published in *The Forge Literary Magazine, Good Men Project* and *Daily Inspired Life*. He graduated from the Newport MFA at Salve Regina University and is working on a book about courage and his incredibly brave son, Justin.

Anthony D'Aries is the author of *The Language of Men: A Memoir*, which received the PEN Discovery Prize and Foreword's Memoir-of-the-Year Award. His work has appeared in *McSweeney's, Boston Magazine, Solstice, Shelf Awareness, The Literary Review, Memoir Magazine, Sport Literate, Flash Fiction Magazine,* and elsewhere. He currently directs the low-residency MFA in Creative and Professional Writing at Western Connecticut State University.

Kelly de la Rocha's work gives voice to what often goes unnoticed: Malawian schoolgirls, empty metal hangers, a woman in a food pantry line, a film container full of marigold seeds. A poet, journalist and editor living in Farmington, her poems have been featured in The Poetry Institute's *Circumference Magazine*, Poetry on the Streets' *Essential Voices from the Pandemic, Gallery and Studio Arts Journal, The Revolution (Relaunch)*, Syracuse Cultural Workers' *Women Artists Datebook* and others.

Kenneth DiMaggio was born in Hartford, raised in New Britain, and educated in a blue collar Cat'lick family and several state universities from Connecticut to Nebraska. He is back again in Connecticut teaching English at Capital Community College in Hartford. He has previously had work published in *Paterson Literary Review, Illuminations, Down in the Dirt,* and *Chiron Review.*

Daniel Donaghy is the author of three poetry collections, most recently *Somerset*, co-winner of the Paterson Poetry Prize, and *Start with the Trouble*, winner of the University of Arkansas Press Poetry Prize.

A lifelong social justice activist, Regina S. Dyton's work is at once personal and political, expressing the array of feelings and experiences in the intersections of identities. Regina is a contributor to the 2020 *Every Kinda' Lady Poetic Anthology* and the June 2021 *Chicken Soup for the Soul* book of writings by African American women. She has presented dramatic readings of her work in several local venues.

Meghan Evans is a native of Hartford, CT. She attended the Greater Hartford Academy of the Arts and earned her B.A. at Trinity College. She earned her M.F.A. in Creative Writing at Sarah Lawrence College. She currently teaches in the English Dept. at CCSU.

James Finnegan has published poems in *Ploughshares, Poetry Northwest, The Southern Review, The Virginia Quarterly Review*, as well as in the anthologies: *Good Poems: American Places* edited by Garrison Keillor; *Laureates of Connecticut; Shadows of Unfinished Things; Imagining Vesalius; Waking Up to the Earth;* and recently *Walkers in the City*. He posts aphoristic ars poetica on the blog *ursprache:* https://ursprache.blogspot.com/

A family therapist and church musician by day, Cathy Fiorello is a voracious reader and scribbler of poems by night. Her poem, *"Little Women* by Louisa May Alcott," was produced in a monthly writing workshop that focuses on 12-Step recovery. She has been published in *Families: the Frontline of Pluralism* and *Ruminate* and is currently seeking an agent for her Contemporary novel, *Dreamreader*. You can follow her at cathyfiorello.com.

Kathryn Fitzpatrick is an MFA student at the University of Alabama with works published or forthcoming in *Hippocampus, Out Magazine, Cleaver Magazine,* and elsewhere. Her micro essay, "Leslie" was longlisted in *Smokelong Quarterly*'s Grand Micro contest. Kathryn is a fourth-generation resident of Thomaston, Connecticut, where she works at a bank.

Sean Frederick Forbes is an Assistant Professor-in-Residence of English and the Director of the Creative Writing Program at the University of Connecticut. His poems have appeared in *Chagrin River Review, Sargasso, A Journal of Caribbean Literature, Language, and Culture, Crab Orchard Review, Long River Review,* and *Midwest Quarterly. Providencia,* his first book of poetry, was published in 2013. He is the poetry editor for *New Square,* the official publication of The Sancho Panza Literary Society.

After years of working for media, higher education and non-profit organizations, Beth Gibbs, M.A., is pursuing her passion to write fiction and nonfiction for mainstream audiences. She uses her energy and sense of humor to inspire, inform, and entertain. She has published a personal growth book titled, *Enlighten Up! Finding Clarity, Contentment and Resilience in a Complicated World* and a children's book, *Ogi Bogi, The Elephant Yogi.* Her personal blog can be found at bethgibbs.com

Margaret Gibson, Poet Laureate of Connecticut, has 13 books of poems, most recently *The Glass Globe*. Awards: the Lamont Selection, Melville Kane Award, the Connecticut Book Award. She was a finalist for the National Book Award, 1993, and for the Poets' Prize, 2016. With a grant from the Academy of American Poets, she edited an anthology, *Waking Up to the Earth: Connecticut Poets in a Time of Global Climate Crisis*. Her website: www.margaretgibsonpoetry.com

Benjamin S. Grossberg's books include *My Husband Would* (University of Tampa Press, 2020), a Foreword INDIES Book of the Year, and *Sweet Core Orchard* (University of Tampa Press, 2009), winner of a Lambda Literary Award. He is Director of Creative Writing at the University of Hartford.

A rising senior in West Hartford, Nora Holmes has been recognized by *The New York Times*, NCTE, and the Scholastic Art and Writing Awards. In 2021, she was a finalist for the Sunken Garden Poetry festival opening for the keynote poet Chen Chen. When not writing, she competes in track and cross country at the regional and national level. Her interests include women's rights, archeology, and her dog: Liam.

Mackenzie Hurlbert is a short fiction writer with previous publications in *Written Tales: Horror, Flash Fiction Magazine, Poor Yorick, Folio Literary Magazine, Five:2:One's The Sideshow*, and *We Walk Invisible*. Her story "Milk Teeth" received honorable mention in the 2019 Writer's Digest Popular Fiction Awards. She studied at Southern Connecticut State University in New Haven, CT and is a proud member of the Northern Connecticut Writer's Workshop.

B. Fulton Jennes is the Poet Laureate of Ridgefield, CT. Her poems have or will appear in the *2020 Connecticut Literary Anthology*, *Comstock Review*, *Tupelo Quarterly*, *Night Heron Barks*, *Tar River Poetry*, *Stone Canoe*, *Vassar Review*, *Connecticut River Journal*, *Naugatuck River Journal*, and many others. In 2021, her poem "From the Room of an Unknown Girl" was awarded the Leslie McGrath Prize. *Blinded Birds*, a chapbook, will be published in spring of 2022.

Christine Kalafus's award-winning manuscript, *Blueprint for Daylight*, a memoir of infidelity, cancer, colicky twins, and the flood in her basement, was excerpted in *Connecticut's Emerging Writers*. Essays have appeared in *Longreads*, *PAGE*, and the *Woven Tale Press*. Her poem "Horses" was the recipient of The Knightville Poetry Award and was nominated for a Pushcart Prize. Christine is an instructor at Westport Writers' Workshop and facilitator of the Quiet Corner chapter of the Connecticut Poetry Society.

A best-selling author and award-winning storyteller, Dr. Raouf Mama is the only one in the world today who tells English, French, Fon and Yoruba folktales from his native Benin and other parts of the world. He is a Distinguished Professor of English at Eastern Connecticut State University. "The Good Samaritan" is part of his debut novel in-progress, *Burning Candles*, a lyrical work of social criticism shot through with magical realism.

Crystal D. Mayo is a writer, actress and mentor for Girl's Write Now. Her memoirs *Teaching You a Lesson*, *The Evolution of Hip Hop*, *Mother to Son*, *Remembering Ma Bea*, and numerous others have been published in *African Voices*, *Our Voices, Our Stories*, *The Bronx Memoir Project Volume III, IV and V*. Her monologue, "Mother to Son," is featured at 08:46 in the anthology for black playwrights, produced by the New World Theater.

Amanda Parrish Morgan's first book, *Stroller*, an examination of cultural attitudes towards parenting and young children, is forthcoming from Bloomsbury's Object Lesson series in 2022. Some of her other essays have appeared in *Guernica*, *The Rumpus*, *The Millions*, *n+1*, *Electric Literature*, *Carve*, *The American Scholar* and the *Ploughshares* Blog. She's also written pieces for *JSTOR Daily*, *The Washington Post*, *Real Simple*, *Women's Running*, and *ESPNW*.

Amy L. Nocton lives in Storrs, Connecticut with her family. She teaches high school Spanish and English composition at the University of Connecticut. When not working, Amy enjoys reading, and visiting with family and friends both in the States and abroad. She has been previously published in *Poetry Ireland Review*, *Ethel Zine*, *Inti,: Revista de literatura hispánica*, *The Bookends Review*, *Dodging the Rain*, and through the Connecticut Writing Project at the University of Connecticut.

Victoria Nordlund is the creative writing director at Rockville High School in Vernon, CT, an adjunct professor at the University of Connecticut, and a lead master teaching artist at The Mark Twain House. Her poetry collections *Wine-Dark Sea* and *Binge Watching Winter on Mute* are published by Main Street Rag. A Best of the Net and Pushcart Prize Nominee, her work has appeared in *PANK Magazine*, *Rust+Moth*, *Chestnut Review*, *Pidgeonholes*, and other journals.

Monica Ong is the author of *Silent Anatomies*, winner of the Kore Press First Book Award in poetry. A Kundiman fellow, Ong has been awarded residencies most recently at Studios at MassMoCA, Military Arts, and Yaddo. Her work has been published in *POETRY Magazine*, *Waxwing Magazine*, *ctrl+v* and forthcoming in *Scientific American*. You can find her visual poetry and objects in the Collection of American Literature at the Yale Beinecke Rare Book & Manuscript Library.

Bessy Reyna, former opinion columnist for the *Hartford Courant*, *Identidad Latina* and contributor to *ctlatinonews.com*. Her work has been published in anthologies in the USA and Latin America. Her book *"Memoirs of the Unfaithful Lover"* is a bilingual poetry collection. She has participated in poetry readings and festivals in the USA and Latin America. She is Bolton's Poet Laureate and recipient of the Lifetime Achievement Award from the CT Center for the Book (www.bessyreyna.com)

Lorraine Riess is a member of Connecticut River Poets, where she participates in group readings at local venues. Her work has appeared in publications and anthologies in the shoreline area. Her first collection of poems is due to be published later this year. She is the current Poet Laureate of Haddam, CT. *Matroyshka Doll* honors women who have chosen not to have children and the pressure that comes from that decision.

Samantha Schwind is a freelance writer and proofreader based in Connecticut. She studied professional writing and psychology at Southern Connecticut State University, as well as publishing and digital media at New York University. Her poetry has appeared on *The New York Times Learning Blog*. In her spare time, Samantha enjoys reading romance novels, writing poetry, binge-watching Netflix dramas, and spending time with her wonderful dog, Ducky.

Wendy Tarry was born and raised in Ottawa, Canada, but now makes her home on the Connecticut shoreline. Tarry holds degrees in English and Education from the University of Ottawa and a Master's in Divinity from Queen's University. Her poem "After the Protest" was published in the Connecticut Literary Anthology 2020. She enjoys working in a local library, assisting with worship at her church, and exploring Connecticut with her husband and their two daughters.

Christopher Torockio is the author of two collections of short stories and two novels, most recently *The Soul Hunters*. His fiction has appeared in *Ploughshares, The Iowa Review, The Gettysburg Review, Colorado Review, The Antioch Review, Denver Quarterly, West Branch, Willow Springs*, and elsewhere. He lives with his wife and son in Willimantic, and teaches at Eastern Connecticut State University.

Brittany Walls is a writer from Milford, who fell in love with poetry at age 10. Despite pursuing other side hustles, she kept coming back to the basics. Aside from poetry, she owns a crocheting business, Zorah UnThreaded LLC, which specializes in self-care and confidence building through crochet. Any way she can express herself and share with others makes her happiest!

Made in USA - Crawfordsville, IN
60214_9781732414167
04.14.2022 1910